SILVER LIGHTS

Michelle Lynn

Published 2019

Printed in the United States of America
Print ISBN: 978-1951490010

Canoe Tree Press
4697 Main Street
Manchester, VT 05255

www.CanoeTreePress.com

Silver Lights and the poem "Dance of Sunshine" is Dedicated to the world of performing arts: dance, music, theatre, film and singing. The book is also in honor of the spirit world and those forgotten dreams. I want to also acknowledge my sister, Laurie who is still alive in spirit and gave me the faith and support in one of my meditations to continue my dreams in the world of performing arts.

Let this story inspire you to dig deep into those childhood dreams, and feel the warmth within and around you, so discovering the magic of *The Silver Lights* can also guide you towards lightness.

As a certified yoga teacher I want to bless you as you continue to follow your dreams. Stay hopeful, be moving and keep following the light.

Namaste from Michelle Lynn

THE DANCE OF SUNSHINE

You could see
The dance had moved
Skylar's
Spirit to ignite Fire as her
Eyes blazed her
Forgotten dreams
Across the stage.
She danced the
Night away, swaying
Her hips,
Opening her wounds, and
Feeling sharpness
From the broken glass.
Her unspoken words became
Her dialogue to Dance into
A Hollywood dream,
Spotlighting
Her New character,
Soleil to tango
In the Sunshine

TABLE OF CONTENTS

CHARACTERS

SKYLAR: HOLLYWOOD DREAMER AND EXOTIC DANCER "SOLEIL"

ANASTASIA: REAL ESTATE COLLEAGUE AND EXOTIC DANCER

SHAY: HOUSE MOM WHO MANAGES DRESSING ROOM AND BACK ROOM OPERATIONS

REDMOND: ASSISTANT MANAGER AT SILVER LIGHTS

DESIREE: SALES ASSOCIATE AT HUSTLER LINGERIE

CHARLIE: BOUNCER AT PENTHOUSE

MRS. KASTLE: SKYLAR'S MIDDLE SCHOOL MATH TEACHER

DONNA: INTERN SUPERVISOR

JAVIER: SKYLAR'S BESTIE AND REAL ESTATE COLLEAGUE

RACHEL: BARTENDER AT PENTHOUSE

BARBIE: EXOTIC DANCER AT PENTHOUSE & REDMOND'S GIRLFRIEND

TONY MURANO: HEAD OF SILVER LIGHTS, KNOWN AS "LION KING"

VICTORIA MARINO: TONY'S GIRLFRIEND & JOHN MARINO'S SISTER

LIV: BARTENDER/SERVER AT SILVER LIGHTS

DJ PAULY: SILVER LIGHTS DJ

LOLA: PREMIERE ENTERTAINER AT SILVER LIGHTS AND ASPIRING FILM DIRECTOR

MICHAEL DONAHUE: GENERAL CHAMPAGNE HOST AT SILVER LIGHTS

FRANKIE MARTINEZ: ASSISTANT CHAMPAGNE HOST AT SILVER LIGHTS

STEVEN BANKS: CEO OF GEMSTONE HOSPITALITY & VENTURES

CHARLES MARZIANO: HEDGE FUND OWNER AND KNOWN AS "THE BEAST OF WALLSTREET", CANIDATE FOR MAYOR 2020

BROOKS KENNEDY: POLITICAL AND SOCIALITE HEIR. OWNER OF ONYX EQUITIES

AMBER RAY: NYC'S BIGGEST PORN STAR AND SILVER LIGHTS' BIGGEST MARKETING TOOL

JOHN MARINO: MANAGING DIRECTOR AT SAPPHIRE INVESTMENTS AND KNOWN AS "BUCK" ON WALL STREET

BRIANNA: EXOTIC DANCER AT SILVER LIGHTS AND ASPIRING SINGER

PHILLIP DELFONTE: EXECUTIVE AT SAPPHIRE INVESTMENTS

CRAIG PETERS: EXECUTIVE AT SAPPHIRE INVESTMENTS

THOMAS MAHOONEY: NYC MAYOR

MARC MELVIN: PRESDIENT OF GRAMERCY REAL ESTATE

MICHAEL KENNEDY: BROOKS KENNEDY'S BROTHER

LOUIS MAZARATI: FINANCIER IN CHARGE OF THE BIGGEST PONZI SCHEME

PIERRE LUCCA: FRENCH SOCIALITE & PLAYBOY

JAKE RYAN: SOCIAL MEDIA CELEB AND INFLUENCER

FRANK DELUCCA: SILENT INVESTOR OF GEMSTONE HOSPITALITY

CAMDEN ROBERTS: VP AT PRECISION INSTRUMENTS

SALVATORE MARZIANO: GANGSTER AND PART OF NEW YORK CITY'S LARGEST CRIME FAMILY

GRACE DONAHUE: FORMER MODEL AND MICHAEL DONAHUE'S WIFE

CASSANDREA DELFONTE: PHIL DELFONTE'S WIFE. HAVING AN AFFAIR WITH SOMEONE AT HER HUSBAND'S RIVAL FIRM, ONYX EQUITIES

BRAD ROSSDALE: PRIVATE TOP NEW YORK CITY INVESTIGATOR

TREY: ANASTASTIA'S BOYFRIEND

EDDIE MAGGIO: CLOSE FRIEND TO MICHAEL DONAHUE AND OWNS NEW YORK CITY CONFIDENTIAL SECURITY

CHAPTER 1
THE PLAYGROUND OF DREAMS

Imagine a Playground of Dreams where each hop, skip, and jump becomes more exciting than the next as you begin to get closer to your visions. These visions begin to animate your dreams, but only if you begin to embrace the surreal qualities of *The Silver Lights*. *The Silver Lights* will fade in and out of your dreams as you begin to go through different acts, scenes, and roles in your life feature. *The Silver Lights* will always be there, whether you realize it or not, waiting to guide you spiritually to enlightenment.

For Skylar Lynn, *The Silver Lights* give her strength to jump over the trials and tribulations placed on her path as she continues to chase her *Hollywood Dreams* in spite of a bleak forecast. *The Silver Lights* guide her heart and soul faithfully towards reaching her vision as she is given a second chance at bringing her god-given talent back to life through the role as an exotic dancer. It is through the surreal qualities of *The Silver Lights* that she is able to see the broken glass representing her shattered dreams, piece by piece, as her dreams come back together. She begins to use the energy from the Lights to prevail in her unusual role, so the role of an exotic dancer becomes more than just a stripper, but a life-changing role. Skylar Lynn is determined in her first feature to create a story of hope in the face of darkness, so she can shine her own light on her broken glass of dreams by sharing part of her dream in her debut as a screenwriter for the screenplay, *The City of Dreams*.

ACT I, SCENE 1
THE DREAM

INT: SCHOOL

FLASHBACK FROM 1993

FADE IN

For Skylar Lynn, her Playground of Dreams came to life in the year of 1993, when playing with a vision of Hollywood became her hop, skip, and jump to her star-studded role. A promising role that explored different scenes with action sequences of figure skating, writing, dancing, acting, cooking, and painting. It was during these scenes that her dreams began to fertilize all of those seeds of hope, so one day she could star in a flourishing role that would spotlight her talent.

Skylar's teenage years were run on autopilot so much that her life felt scripted. Her days in her role as a teenager demanded much of her time to homework, figure skating lessons, and social events. Her tedious homework assignments and strenuous figure skating practices left her little time to explore her true passion, the field of creative arts.

One day during math class as the window was open and the sunshine flooded in, a magnetic light reflecting off the natural light came into her vision. The light was subtle yet strong enough to magnetize her eyes. The Silver Light began to glimmer with intensity, so much her mind, body, and spirit felt the magical powers. The light reassured her that her dreams were real and that not even the darkest scenes could overpower that. This was the first of many Silver Lights that would ultimately guide her towards her biggest dream of writing and starring in her first screenplay, The City of Dreams. She realized quickly that The Silver Lights would flicker on and off in scenes that didn't illuminate her dreams, most often pertaining to classes like math, history, and geology. However, the illuminating qualities of The Silver Lights appeared in her daydreams of studying visual and performing arts, so perhaps one day she could live out her real dream of becoming an "artist." It was during these classes like math and history that she would automatically fall into a daydream until the sound of her name, "Skylar," would echo across the classroom, and wake her up to reality.

Skylar is daydreaming in her freshman year math class and is woken up by the loud voice of her math teacher and her chalk on the board.

The math teacher, Mrs. Kastle, in her mid-to-late forties, dressed like she was from the 80s in a bright floral dress with frosted blonde hair and overly tan skin. She liked to find at least one student a week to pick on, and it happened to be Skylar this week. She had a reputation for sending kids to detention and embarrassing them.

DIALOGUE

MRS. KASTLE: Now moving on to problem number five. Do you know the answer to question five from the homework assignment?

SKYLAR: It's 250.

MATH TEACHER: Wrong answer. That is the answer to question seven. This is the second time this week that I have caught you dozing off.

SKYLAR: It won't happen again. I'm just tired. I have been getting up early for figure skating.

Skylar's homework is buried amongst the US Weekly. *She is trying to cover up the magazine without making it too obvious. The teacher walks all the way to the back of the classroom and grabs the* US Weekly.

MATH TEACHER: That's not an excuse. What's this?

SKYLAR: It's part of my English assignment.

Her classmates begin to laugh and chuckle.

MATH TEACHER: An English assignment for US *Weekly*? Come on, you really think I'm going to buy into this lie? (*She holds the magazine up and then turns to the pages.*) Well, this story looks interesting about Tom Cruise and Nicole Kidman. Is that a heart around Tom?

SKYLAR: What?

CLASS: (*Noise and laughter*)

MATH TEACHER: Quiet. Skylar I want you to go to the principal's office and explain your US *Weekly* English Lit assignment to him.

In shock, but still composed, Skylar excused herself from the classroom, and as she left the classroom she went back into her scripted role as she entered the principal's office.

Her scripted role in these mandatory classes like chemistry, math, and history just about paused her dialogue in every scene of The Dream. It was during these early years that she realized her joy and inspiration came from her dreams that she was the next Audrey Hepburn from Breakfast at Tiffany's or Jennifer Grey from Dirty Dancing.

At thirteen, Skylar's unscripted role left her hungry for a taste of innovation as she began to fuel up on creativity by performing on all of her favorite sets: the kitchen, the ice skating rink, the arts and crafts room, the stage, and the production studio. You can see how the flavor of innovation affected her aura. The light in her almond-shaped eyes sparkled with magic, her long, wavy, coffee-colored hair glistened in the light, and her petite frame became bigger than life as she began to explore her dream in the year of 1993.

The year of 1993 was the first time she got a real taste of excitement from her unscripted role. On the other hand, the constant noise outside The Playground of Dreams began to pause the early stages of preproduction on The City of Dreams. It was during her teenage years that the noise outside The Playground of Dreams began to muffle her creativity in the field of art, leaving her once again torn between two roles: one as a scripted extra in the setting of Cleveland, Ohio, or the other one as a dreamer on the set of The City of Dreams.

FADE OUT

ACT I, SCENE 2
THE JUNGLE GYM OF DREAMS

FLASHBACK FROM 1998 TO 2012

FADE IN

The spotlight of The Silver Lights began to flicker in and out during the year of 1998. Skylar was in her senior year of high school, and she was facing one of the biggest decisions yet: whether to pursue a college degree or to go off path and take the route less explored, which would be pursuing a path in the arts.

Skylar's character wanted just to abandon the scripted role she inherited, and head in the opposite direction with no script, just her Dream. The more Skylar thought about her dream as a Hollywood Artist, the more she visualized herself flying away from her inherited role and into something far different. Still, Skylar's fear got the best of her during this time, and instead of exploring her dreams, she went towards the route of college.

Over the next twelve years, Skylar's character played around in The Jungle Gym of Dreams, always stuck between two roles, one free with no lines or heavy costumes, and one tied down to a script.

Her role began to come alive in between those takes as she began to see her own talent from magnetic force of The Silver Lights, which showed her character the gift of art when it came to writing, acting, and storytelling. The Silver Lights gave her the energy to discover her talent for storytelling and acting. Each time a flashback from The Jungle Gym of Dreams would enter her vision, Skylar would begin to transcend her darkest moments by starting to write and visualize her dreams as a leading lady starring in her first written screenplay, The City of Dreams.

FADE OUT

ACT I, SCENE 3
ALL THE WORLD'S A STAGE

INT: CLEVELAND PLAYHOUSE

FLASHBACK FALL 2003

FADE IN

As Shakespeare said, "All the world's a stage, and all the men and women merely players." This became Skylar's motto after college graduation. Her opening lines softly faded into the mute landscape of her grey cubicle, yet her closing lines projected loudly across her worldly stage as she entered The Cleveland Playhouse, once again splitting her center stage with different character sets, takes, and lines.

Skylar's role during this time period had many exits and entrances leading to different scenes. One notable scene was her debut in her film class at The Cleveland Playhouse, where she learned about fundamentals for acting on camera. Skylar started to have recurring flashbacks of her hop, skip, and jump from her Playground of Dreams, reverting back in time to her eighth grade studio production class. It was during this class she felt her spirit come alive. You can see the production element revived her tired spirit, bringing curiosity to her lines, excitement to her dialogue, and character to her face.

The second scene in "All the World's a Stage" was shot during her role as an intern at American Greetings. It was the year 2003; she had just graduated college, her days of sorority rush, and late-night pizza runs faded into the drone-like culture of corporate America. Her new role as an intern felt more like a robot working endlessly to do the same tasks every day, including stuffing boxes, sorting greeting cards, and taking orders. The monotony of this routine began to dim her spotlight of hope for any starring roles in her feature, The City of Dreams. The deeper she immersed herself in her role as The Intern from merchandising cards to excel spreadsheets she still managed to see the The Silver Lights.

DIALOGUE

Donna was an overly controlling boss in her upper 30s. She looked like an overweight news anchor and was on her way up to the top. Her style was micromanaging her employees, especially her interns. She would catch Skylar daydreaming in corporate meetings and mundane tasks.

DONNA (INTERN SUPERVISOR): Did you get all the notes for the Valentine holiday assortment?

SKYLAR: I have it all right here. I'm going to get right to the Excel sheets and diagrams for the new holiday setup.

DONNA: Great. I'm just going to skim over your notes to make sure you did not miss anything.

She scrolls through Skylar's notes, finds a lot of stuff missing, and then turns to the back page of her notebook. She finds what appears to be a vision board and sketches.

DONNA: "You are missing the end cap highlights for the greeting cards, and this nonsense about dreams, the beach, and being a movie star. What is all this? This is a work notebook. You should not be scribbling or writing nonsense.

SKYLAR: It's called a vision board. That was when I first started. It won't happen again.

DONNA: Ok, it better not because your future here will be non-existent.

SKYLAR: Non-existent.

DONNA: You know what I'm talking about. You won't have a career here, and if I were you I would forget about those crazy dreams of living by the beach and being a movie star. They don't happen to people like us. You are a small-town girl, and nothing more. You should be happy to have a position here based on your talent, rather than dreaming for something that is not in your cards.

This was one of the first of many that Skylar was told she would not amount to much, and she should be happy with her current role. Over the next ten years her scenes in corporate America paused her production on *The City of Dreams*.

FADE OUT

CHAPTER 2
THE BROKEN GLASS

The sound of broken glass shook the center stage of *The City of Dreams*, shifting the role of Skylar backstage. What felt like a bad dream became a tragedy to Skylar's character. Her shattered dreams of becoming a Hollywood star were instantaneously washed away into the dirty gutter. The fragments from the shattered glass represented parts of Skylar's broken spirit. The sound of the broken glass left the small-town girl in shock as she began to swallow her own fear, leaving her stranded on the empty streets of *The City of Dreams*.

ACT II, SCENE 1
EMPTY STREETS

YEAR: 2015

EXT: CITY OF DREAMS

New York City

FADE IN

The dialogue of The City of Dreams shifts tone as the sound of shattered glass moves her script out of rehearsal and into a solemn dialogue. The sound of the shattered glass rips apart Skylar's dreams, destroying her faith. The scattered glass begins to disrupt her monologue in this act, as Skylar's heart began to beat slower and slower until she becomes helpless, leaving her role in anguish. The empty streets from The City of Dreams becomes darker and more isolated, as her shadows of doubt contrast any light of hope. She continues to walk aimlessly on the empty streets with no set role, script, or direction until she comes to a vintage art inspired café. She stops in and gets a cup of coffee and then sits down. The streets are quiet and empty, and the café is in its last hour before closing. Skylar takes a seat and then begins to take out a few bills, one of them being an eviction notice. She looks down at the bill and notices a two-week period she has to catch up, otherwise she will be out on the empty streets. She looks around and realizes that it's just her and no one else. She begins to try to make sense of her situation.

DIALOGUE

SKYLAR: I would have never dreamed I would be broke, just getting by, working two dead-end jobs in my thirties, and living in a shithole. I really thought the higher power had a better plan for me. Why me? Why couldn't this happen to someone else? I don't deserve this. I'm a pretty good person. I don't lie, steal, cheat, or avoid paying taxes. I don't deserve this eviction notice. I really thought my scenes in *The City of Dreams* would be differently written. Instead, the sound of the broken glass has woken up parts of my broken soul. Now I must gather the most broken parts and put the pieces back together. I must search for a better role in *The City of Dreams*. I'm not going to let my darkest moment get the best of me. I'm going to find the light (*takes a deep breath and closes her eyes*). Higher power, please protect me and help me see the light to guide me out of darkness. Please show me a sign.

All of sudden from out of nowhere, The Silver Lights, a radiant ray of light, projecting right in front of Skylar's table, comes shining through. Skylar is speechless and looks like she saw a ghost.

FADE OUT

ACT II, SCENE 2
THE STARVING ARTIST

INT: NYC STUDIO APARTMENT

FADE IN

Inside the set of her NYC studio, there was a wardrobe chair awaiting her transition to the "Starving Artist." The blue and grey shadows from her makeup vanished as she changed out of her costume from The Playground of Dreams. It was this costume change, along with pieces of the shattered glass, that ultimately would change both her future role and direction in The City of Dreams.

Behind the scenes she began to struggle with the role of The Starving Artist. Her apartment mirrored the setting for one: outdated fixtures from the 1950s, including a vinyl checkered kitchen floor, pipes peeking through the ceiling, cracks in the floor, a pink bathtub, and a miniature kitchen that only had space for a small stovetop and a mini fridge.

You can see her kitchen cupboard was stocked with canned foods and her fridge had only energy drinks and water. In one corner of the tiny apartment, you could see a pile of laundry that had been building up for weeks, and in the other corner there were papers from different companies that she had applied to or worked at throughout the years. *Everything in her tiny New York City apartment had painted "A Portrait of a Starving Artist," including her physical appearance. Skylar's attractive looks on center stage often got her extra attention in between the takes of The City of Dreams; however, inside her apartment, behind the makeup and costume, her Mediterranean features and striking physique looked run down. You can see the dark blue circles under her doe eyes, the frailty in her thin frame, the brassiness in her long hair, and the loss of color in her olive complexion. Her dreams of becoming a leading star in The City of Dreams were cut short as she continued to skip out on rehearsals.*

After many skipped rehearsals, she was left hopeless, withering away like her run-down apartment. With no savings and two dead-end jobs that couldn't meet her expenses, Skylar's spotlight on her silence became vividly real as her struggle was no longer a line or narration in her head, but a harsh reality. You can see her role as an extra in The City of Dreams dwindle to almost nothing as she fought hard to stand on her own two feet again and regain the power of her voice in The City of Dreams.

FADE OUT

CHAPTER 3
THE SOUR APPLE

No one goes to The Big Apple expecting to get a taste of The Sour Apple, instead, one moves there with high hopes that all their dreams will come true. The sweet temptation that entices over 265,000 people to move each year to New York City doesn't taste sweet to everyone. This happened to be the case for the small-town girl, Skylar Lynn. The sweet craving of fashion week, art shows, night club openings, film castings, and noteworthy mentions on *Page Six* of *The Post* left Skylar hungry for a bite of the Big Apple!

At the prime age of thirty, Skylar decided to satisfy her hunger by relocating to The Big Apple for a bite of corporate America. She initially moved for a corporate job that didn't reflect the image from the glass or the vision from the flickering *Silver Light*. The flavor of the Big Apple became sour not long after she took her corporate job. From aggressive New Yorkers who pushed her off the subway to piling bills and long, arduous hours in the cubicle, she had no time to hop, skip, and jump around *The Playground of Dreams*.

Skylar's dialogue went from hopeful and poised to broken up and sad, making her current role impossible to play. Overworked in a low-paying marketing job with no friends, savings, or time to explore *The City of Dreams*, Skylar had no choice but to explore the role of an extra behind the scenes.

The sour taste from *The City of Dreams* began to ruin her appetite so much that the corporate job she had moved for initially began to crumble within weeks before her own eyes, therefore shifting her scenes into the next act, "Survival of The Fittest." Barely getting by, her aspirations for playing a leading lady in *The City of Dreams* began to taste sour as she fought to keep her story going in the act of "Survival of the Fittest."

ACT II, SCENE 3
SURVIVAL OF THE FITTEST

YEAR: 2015

INT: REAL ESTATE OFFICE

FADE IN

Typically speaking, after moving to New York City, within a year there is a small percentage of transplants who can swear the Big Apple still tastes good. On the flip side, there are hundreds of thousands who feel the tug of war on surviving in New York City, and many of these individuals typically come from small towns and humble beginnings. For Skylar Lynn she was a statistic, and she began to feel the hunger pangs from her City of Dreams as she entered her most difficult act yet, "Survival of The Fittest."

It was the year 2015, and the rotten flavor was starting to ruin her taste for any possible starring roles in The City of Dreams. Skylar was hanging on by a thread, struggling to maintain three jobs: a real estate agent, an independent style consultant, and a trade show model. All these jobs combined barely paid her rent. Her weeks were packed with running around chasing down real estate leads, working on last-minute styling assignments, and representing brands at the New York Convention Center.

In reality, her real estate job looked nothing like the hit show Million Dollar Listing, rather a story of a modern-day Cinderella, who, instead of waiting for her Prince Charming, was waiting for her starring role to be handed to her. Those lucrative million-dollar listings and big payouts were nowhere to be found. Skylar quickly learned that the world of New York City real estate mirrored a real life drama full of lies, deceit, nepotism, and long, drawn-out transactions that took months to clear. Her role as a New York City real estate agent left Skylar starving and hungrier for a newer role in The City of Dreams.

It was in this act that Skylar started to feel the need to scour castings for a completely new role, one that would allow her spotlight to overpower her shattered dreams.

She began to search online ads every day in pursuit of something that would allow her to pick the pieces up from the broken glass. You name it, and she clicked on it, including personal assistant, event manager, makeup artist, bottle host, inside sales rep, dog-sitter, and the list goes on. She kept searching diligently, day and night for two weeks until one day in her real estate office, she came across the advertisement, "Upscale Establishment Seeking All Positions."

Skylar's curiosity led her to click the advertisement, which read as:

ADVERTISEMENT

"Silver Lights"– New York City's premiere Gentlemen's Club is hiring dancers. Are you fun, in great shape, outgoing, and just overall great to be around? Then we want you as a premiere dancer and entertainer!!

Are you ready to pay off those bills? APPLY NOW

Are you thinking about going back to school or pursuing a dream? APPLY NOW

Do you need to set your own schedule? APPLY NOW

Are you in the process of changing careers? APPLY NOW

Stop in any night of the week between 9:00 and 11:30 PM. Come be a part of the best nightlife of New York City...

Gazing at the advertisement, Skylar was unaware that her colleague Anastasia was right behind her. Anastasia, a bubbly yet assertive blonde in her early thirties, had curves in all the right places. She saw the advertisement as Skylar noticed a shadow peering over her, and without hesitation she clicked on her bookmark page of favorites.

DIALOGUE

ANASTASIA: Skylar, is everything ok?

SKYLAR: Everything is fine. Why?

ANASTASIA: I just noticed the past month you look a bit stressed. You haven't been yourself. Not to mention you look like you're losing the J. Lo . . . (*Points to the behind.*)

SKYLAR: Oh, no. I can't be losing my behind. (*Laughs.*) Don't tell me that. Have you ever heard of "The Big Apple Diet?"

ANASTASIA: What exactly is it?

(*jokingly but serious*)

SKYLAR: "The Big Apple Diet" is canned soup, Starbucks, Harmony Energy Drinks, and happy hour specials below fifteen dollars.

ANASTASIA: (*sarcastically*) Wow, too good to be true! I definitely need some of that. My ten-year reunion is right around the corner, and all those open-house parties have been packing on the pounds.

SKYLAR: You need to wear my shoes, or should I say "slippers" for a while so you can get a real flavor of "The Big Apple Diet."

ANASTASIA: Skylar, I'm not clueless to struggle. It's not all *Sex and the City* for me, either.

SKYLAR: I never implied it was. I'm not wearing your swanky shoes, so I can't make that call.

ANASTASIA: Oh, you mean these babies? They are TJ Maxx, Michael Kors on clearance. Did you know when I came to the Big Apple I had a black eye, a hundred dollars in my account, and nowhere to call home except a hostel until I had enough money to find an address? Maybe one day I can tell you more.

SKYLAR: (*She looks at Anastasia with curiosity and compassion*) That would be nice.

ANASTASIA: Getting back to your listings and clients, are you ok with the work load?

SKYLAR: Yes, Ana, I am.

ANASTASIA: Great, and I have good news.

SKYLAR: What might that be?

ANASTASIA: We may be getting Steven Banks's business for buying buildings.

SKYLAR: The guy from Gemstone Hospitality who owns the largest hospitality firm in all of New York City.

ANASTASIA: Yes, but don't start spreading rumors. It's on the back burner. We will know more in the next week from Marc Melvin, the president. By the way, how is the Gramercy listing? And have you followed up with the Michael Kennedy lead?

SKYLAR: It's moving along. I'm going to get back to the Gramercy listing today, and I am following up with Michael Kennedy to see if he is interested in the loft I showed him.

ANASTASIA: Great, it sounds like you have your hands ful.

SKYLAR: Sounds good.

The music from her colleague's desk played louder, and it took Skylar's concentration back to the advertisement on the screen.

BACK TO THE ADVERTISEMENT ON THE SCREEN

Paralyzed with fear, she couldn't believe she was considering becoming a stripper. The internal fear that ran through her veins as she peered at the advertisement took on a new face she didn't know existed. She felt trapped in a Twilight Zone, reminiscing visions from The Playground of Dreams. In and out, the light began to flicker in her trance, silently guiding Skylar Lynn towards The Silver Lights.

Would The Silver Lights be strong enough to give Skylar the strength to move out from behind the scenes as an extra and into a leading role that would remove the dialogue of fear, spotlighting her gift of "words" in her first written screenplay, The City of Dreams?

Skylar knew if she didn't act quickly, her story in The City of Dreams would be paused, and her character would just wither away to nothing. Down to her survivor instincts with only 100 dollars in her account and just enough canned food stacked for the week, she started to pray to her highest power for answers. She slowly began to close her eyes, listening to each inhale and exhale, mustering enough strength to ease the burden of her struggles. With each inhale, she began to breathe courage, letting go of her struggles as The Silver Lights began to permeate her aura, fading her deepest fears, and wiping away her burdens. The Silver Lights began to solidify her prayers, guiding her voice towards the role of a lifetime, one that would ultimately dance her way into "A Hollywood Dream."

FADE OUT

CHAPTER 4
THE ROLE OF A LIFETIME

Everyone dreams of the day he or she lands the role of a lifetime. The role in your heart you were destined for, the one you have been dreaming of since you could talk. These roles change your entire purpose on earth and oftentimes test your faith, patience, perseverance, and dignity, and push you into your own feature story that will bring upon *The Silver Lights*.

For Skylar Lynn, the role of a lifetime was awaiting her as she was getting ready to audition in a New York City gentlemen's club called Silver Lights. This role would test her faith, perseverance, dignity, and purpose so much that she would finally feel the magic powers of *The Silver Lights*. For Skylar Lynn, the power of her own silence allowed her to finally take the first few steps towards the foreign world of Silver Lights.

ACT III, SCENE 1
THE AUDITION

INT: SILVER LIGHTS DRESSING ROOM

FADE IN

As Skylar stood in line awaiting her turn, she began to get butterflies in her stomach. You can see the sweat on her forehead, the fear in her coffee-colored eyes, and the anxiety building up in her smile. Fear began to paralyze Skylar Lynn as she continued to let her thoughts run rampant about being topless on stage.

From out of nowhere, the name "Skylar" echoed in the empty club. The voice was coming from House Mom, Shelia, known as Shay around Silver Lights. A former beauty queen and dancer, who after ten years of dancing retired to the backstage. This included managing all dance auditions, orientations, and conflicts with both new and older entertainers. Shelia had a thick Spanish accent and looked like a Barbie doll from head to toe: perfectly manicured nails, flawless makeup, and flashy jewelry. She had moved from Colombia to America after she retired from her beauty pageant days in hopes of a better life. Shortly after arriving, she found herself struggling to keep up with her basic necessities like rent and food, and fell into the path of dancing to survive as a single mom. You can see she took *pride in her job, and her motherly instinct and warm demeanor just shined with everyone that that she came in contact with, earning her reputation as an angel at Silver Lights.*

Skylar noticed the golden aura of the House Mom immediately.

She walked to the front of the dressing room and continued to look lost.

DIALOGUE

SHAY: Can you look over your application one more time to make sure everything is correct?

SKYLAR: (*She looks it over quickly*) (*Nervously*) Everything is good.

SHAY: Your application states that you have no prior experience dancing at any other gentlemen's club.

SKYLAR: Yes ma'am, that is correct.

SHAY: Please call me Shay. That's my nickname at Silver Lights. I'm the main person here if you have any personal issues that interfere with this job or an issue among the dancers. I keep the peace here and have been for over twenty years doing various jobs from dancer to host manager and now as house mom. If you do get hired, I'm here to guide you. Do you have any questions before the audition?

SKYLAR: How long is it?

SHAY: The audition is a three-minute song. The first minute, you dance on stage with the dress. The second minute you take off the dress in a subtle way with the dance, and the remainder of the time you dance topless with the music until the manager, Redmond, signals you to come off. He will let me know if it's a "Go" or "No." If you are hired, you will continue to fill out the paperwork, and I will go over rules, operations, and policies. Then either Redmond or the floor host will walk you through the club explaining how dances work, how we sell VIP rooms, and the expectation at *Silver Lights*. It's a lot to hear all at once. Do you have questions?

SKYLAR: What do we wear for the audition?

SHAY: You have to wear t-back underwear that we sell here. (*She points to the underwear and dress area*).

SKYLAR: I'll go get dressed.

Skylar is holding a black corporate-type dress in her hand to change into.

SHAY: You're not wearing that. (*Points to Skylar's corporate-looking dress*)

SKYLAR: Yes, I am. Is there a problem with this?

SHAY: It looks like you're going to a party for Trump.

SKYLAR: (*flushed and embarrassed*) Ok, I will toss the dress. How much is that dress going for? (*She points to a shiny coral spandex tube dress*)

SHAY: It's sixty dollars with tax, and I will throw in the t-back for free since you are buying a dress. Let me know when you're finished getting dressed and your hair and makeup is all done. I will then walk you to the Stage of Dreams.

SKYLAR: Stage of Dreams?

SHAY: Yes, it's the way I view the stage. It's a way to dance towards your daydreams.

SKYLAR: I like that analogy. I would have never thought a gentlemen's club with a pole would be a place for someone to dance towards their daydreams.

SHAY: One last thing. Have you had any jobs that you feel can relate to being an exotic dancer? (*Looks down at the application, and then up at Skylar*).

SKYLAR: I was Miller Lite Ambassador for nightlife. The closest to performing for dancing would be that I was a figure skater when I was younger. Right now I have been doing Zumba a few days a week at New York City Sports Club, but I haven't had much experience in this industry.

SHAY: (*Laughs*) Skylar, all that is great, but working at a premiere club like Silver Lights is different than being a promotional model for a beer company or doing Zumba! Just remember to relax and listen to the music as you take to the "Stage of Dreams."

FADE OUT

ACT III, SCENE 2
THE DANCE AUDITION

INT: SILVER LIGHTS CLUB

FADE IN

House Mom Shay directs Skylar outside the dressing room towards the side entrance of the center stage. From the moment you walk into Silver Lights, the atmosphere resembles a Winter Wonderland: glass block designs, crystal chandeliers in front, and silver flooring. As you enter the main room of the club, patrons are ordering drinks at the side of bar. Inside the club, the main area has four sections: the main bar area, the main seating area, the back seating area and the three stages. Inside the main room there are three stages, and the interior theme implies eroticism with red lights reflecting against the dark red upholstery, posters of semi-naked entertainers around the club. The carpet is a dark grey, and the seating is upholstered with lush red velour coverings and charcoal gray tables that each have a Silver Lights drink menu. There is dark red drapery from above the ceiling and all over the club to reflect the red-light ambience of "erotica." Behind the bar, the glass-block design was plastered across the wall so much that it looked like an ice fortress. The bar was stacked with every type of liquor, beer, and wine imaginable.

The night manager, Redmond, a young Charlie Hunnam type, greeted Skylar with a southern accent. Immediately, his rugged looks and southern charm calmed her nerves.

DIALOGUE

REDMOND: Hi, Skylar, I'm Redmond. It's a pleasure to meet you.

SKYLAR: Same. (*nervously*)

REDMOND: I'm assuming Shay went over the audition. We are going to start you after this song. Our audition process is different in that we do all the auditions in front of the crowd. Is there anything you need to ask before you go on?

SKYLAR: So, if I'm correct, the top comes off in the last minute of the song.

REDMOND: It sure does, beautiful. Just relax, and I'm sure you will do fine.

A new song came on over the speaker, signaling Skylar to begin her audition. She took a deep breath and began to exhale her deepest fears of dancing topless. She awkwardly walked to the center stage, praying her performance would be satisfactory so she could start immediately and make money to cover her piling bills. As she stepped onstage, a deeper power began to take over, and just like that *The Silver Lights* began to enter her vision, guiding her performance. Right away her aura changed. You can see her fear fade away as the light in her eyes begins to sparkle, and the color in her skin begins to glow. The rhythm of the music begins to uplift her spirit to a new dimension she didn't know existed. You can see the way she sways her hips, moves her feet, and dances with the music; her life begins to take on possibility. With each new beat she begins to breathe and visualize an award-winning performance that would pick up the pieces of her shattered dreams.

The beats of the music begin to pick up as she is down to the last minute of her audition, reminding her she needs to become topless. All of sudden, her heart begins to beat faster than possible, but once again *The Silver Lights* reappear shining light on her anxiety. The light begins to calm her nerves as she removes her dress with ease. The panic she had experienced before the audition disappeared as her new role awaiting her would forever change her life.

FADE OUT

ACT III, SCENE 3
WELCOME "SOLEIL"

INT: DRESSING ROOM

FADE IN

The dressing room was starting to fill up with dancers. The loud chatter, outrageous stories, heavy makeup applications, and flashy costumes all resembled a circus that Skylar would soon be joining. Skylar was astonished that she danced topless in front of strangers for the first time ever. Lost in a trance, she was awoken by the sweet voice of House Mom Shay.

DIALOGUE

SHAY: Skylar, I have great news. First off, a big congrats! (*She hugs Skylar.*) I want to welcome you to Silver Lights. You are family now.

SKYLAR: Wow. I can't believe it. I'm really an exotic dancer.

SHAY: Yes, you are, and it's going to change your life for sure in a good way. In the meantime, I need you to fill out the paperwork, and I will go over some procedures for checking in and getting on the floor, the duration of your shifts, and the expectations. You will start two days from now, so Wednesday will be your first night. You will be paired up with Lola for the week. She is our top champagne seller and has a stellar reputation here with customers and staff. You can watch how she talks to the customers, how she dances, and how she sells VIP rooms at the club. I know it's a lot of information, but once you're on the floor dancing, you will pick it up. Do you have any questions?

SKYLAR: None at this time. Thank you.

SHAY: Here is the paperwork I need you to fill out and get started. Please read through our rules, procedures, and expectations. As you read, you will notice the sections: Dress Code, Grooming, Compensation, VIP Rooms, and Dances. Please pay extra close attention to these sections, and you have to pick a stage name. The stage name is an alias to protect your private life. Do you have any that come to mind?

SKYLAR: Soleil.

SHAY: That's a beautiful name. Welcome, Soleil! What is the meaning?

SKYLAR: It means "sun" in French.

SHAY: Beautiful. I love French food, not to mention French men are the best lovers, even over Greek men.

SKYLAR: So Greek men are second?

SHAY: You know the old myth that all the hunky men were Greek gods and descendants from that culture, but if you ask me, French men are not only better lovers, but are better chefs!

SKYLAR: I have not yet dated a Greek or French man. I have only had experience with the Italian stallions.

SHAY: Forget the Italian stallions—they gallop away when things don't go their way. French men just get better with time, and they melt your heart. Speaking of French men, there is a hunky customer who goes by the name Pierre Luca that will make your jaw drop and give you butterflies in your stomach. His French accent will bait you, and then his piercing blue eyes will hook you. Trust me, there is something about him and his devilishly handsome looks that will lure you in.

SKYLAR: So, if I hear a French accent by a super hot looking guy, then I need to get excited?

SHAY: Get excited, but be yourself with him because he reads past those dancers that are just looking to take advantage of him. He is genuine and will make it rain on you if he likes you. He is also known to be a knight in shining armor outside the club.

SKYLAR: Outside the club?

SHAY: Some girls decide to date their customers. That is completely up to you, but do not talk about it here at the club. We prefer you don't see customers outside the club.

SKYLAR: Understood. It doesn't surprise me about French men. They are the best chefs, and you know that a man that is good in the kitchen is obviously good in the bedroom.

SHAY: (*Laughs.*) Soleil, I love your sense of humor. (*Phone rings.*) I'm going to take this call. If you have any questions with the application, let me know.

FADE OUT

The lighthearted conversation and humor between Skylar and House Mom Shay calmed Skylar's nerves; however, she still had so many thoughts running through her head as she began to read the policies, procedures, and details of her new role at Silver Lights. Would her fears choke her so she wouldn't be able to speak, and how would she be able to compete with the other beautiful dancers for the same customers? Would she fit in at Silver Lights or stick out like a sore thumb? All these thoughts were running through her head as she began to read the sections. It wasn't until she read the expectations of the VIP rooms, stage dancing, and table dances that she started to feel frozen in her new role as the exotic dancer, "Soleil".

CHAPTER 5
THE EXOTIC DANCER

Little did Skylar know that the role she would embark on in her future scenes would be more than a wardrobe change, but one that would forever impact her character. Skylar's everyday wardrobe consisted of skinny jeans, simple tops, flat shoes, minimal makeup, and straight hair. Nothing about Skylar's current wardrobe screamed "sexy" or "exotic dancer." Her everyday street look was casual but trendy: a pair of skinny jeans to show off her petite frame, fashion boots to give her look a modern feel, and a boho-inspired top that spoke Skylar's personality. She had two days to get her act down for playing the role of Soleil, the exotic dancer. Due to the time constraints of her three other jobs, a real estate agent, a trade show model, and a styling consultant, there wasn't much time in between to prepare.

Would Skylar be able to adapt to her new role, dialogue, wardrobe, and direction without hesitation? All these questions soon would be answered in the upcoming acts as Skylar Lynn began to prepare for her first day performing as "Soleil," the exotic dancer.

ACT IV, SCENE 1
THE COSTUME OF A STRIPPER

INT: HUSTLER LINGERIE STORE

FADE IN

A nervous Skylar is walking around the adult section browsing the sex toys and lingerie as a young saleswoman in her twenties with shoulder-length blonde hair and big boobs approaches her.

DIALOGUE

SALES ASSOCIATE DESIREE: Are you finding everything ok? I'm Desiree. We have some great deals going on among the fetish section and role play costumes.

SKYLAR: Role play costumes?

SALES ASSOCIATE DESIREE: Yes, costumes for role play are a big part of the adult industry. They create fantasy, which is one element in the business of fetish parties, gentlemen's clubs, and swinger parties. Do you want me to show you our top-selling one? The dominatrix one?

SKYLAR: Nah, I'm not ready to be a dominatrix. I would prefer to be a submissive.

SALES ASSOCIATE DESIREE: Really? You're missing out because it's so fun, and a lot of high-powered men at the end of the day just want to give up control and be dominated.

SKYLAR: (*Hesitantly*) Okay. I just came in looking for some dresses or lingerie.

SALES ASSOCIATE DESIREE: So are you a porn star, stripper, or starved housewife that needs to get laid?

SKYLAR LYNN: (*laughs*) I'm an exotic dancer. (*Embarrassed*) I just got hired.

SALES ASSOCIATES: Peaches, there is no need to be embarrassed about that. I help lots of young women like yourself turn into exotic dancers, if you prefer to use that word over "strippers."

SKYLAR LYNN: That's good to hear because I literally just got hired yesterday at Silver Lights, and I start Wednesday. And I have no clue what I should wear.

SALES ASSOCIATE DESIREE: I sell a lot of lingerie, club wear, and other accessories to all types of dancers, including experienced and newbies like yourself.

SKYLAR: Great, can you give me a few suggestions and point me towards a couple of outfits that I can wear?

SALES ASSOCIATE DESIREE: Sure thing.

The sales associate takes Skylar towards the club dresses and racy lingerie, and also points towards the shoe section, specifically the silver heels.

SALES ASSOCIATE DESIREE: All the girls at Silver Lights have at least one club dress and a solid color teddy with stockings, and they all own a pair of silver heels.

SKYLAR: Stockings? You mean the ones I wear under dresses?

SALES ASSOCIATE DESIREE: No. (*Giggles.*) Wow, you really are new to this. Let the naughty adventure begin.

SKYLAR: Naughty adventure?

SALES ASSOCIATE DESIREE: Yes, it's just a term I use for amateurs who are new to the adult industry. Let's get back to the costume that you will be wearing. First off, stockings are like candy to the men as they come in. Some stockings look sweeter than others, so it gets them horny so they are ready to get teased through a dance.

SKYLAR: Really . . . (*Nods her head innocently.*)

SALES ASSOCIATE DESIREE: Yes, it gets certain customers' jaws dropping.

SKYLAR: Okay. I guess I will try on that black teddy and the hot pink club dress. I will also take a black lace pair of stockings.

SALES ASSOCIATE DESIREE: Great. I will get the stuff, and you can go to the dressing room. Peaches, it's that way. And one last thing, what size shoe do you wear?

SKYLAR: Size eight.

SALES ASSOCIATE DESIREE: I'm going to grab you a pair of silver heels to go with your look. The silver heels are a must for your wardrobe. They not only complete the whole look but will help you sparkle and shine when you dance. Just remember, let your silver heels connect with the rhythm of your spirit, not just the music.

SKYLAR: Thanks. I get that concept because I practice yoga, but I still feel a little clueless to playing the role of an exotic dancer.

SALES ASSOCIATE DESIREE: Honey, you will learn. Stop stressing yourself out. A long time ago I, too, was new to this world. You're not alone. (*She looks at Skylar with a silent understanding. She pauses. Someone walks in the door.*) I need to go to the front.

Skylar goes to the dressing room. She takes a deep breath and calms herself down. She closes her eyes to begin a deep meditation. She begins to pray and ask her higher power to get her through the next few days. She proceeds to get dressed in her first black teddy lingerie. The sales associate knocks on the door and says she has the silver heels. She slides them under the door. Skylar puts the silver heels on and then begins to imagine how they will elevate her new role as "A Star" by connecting her mind, body, and spirit.

FADE OUT

CHAPTER 6
A STAR

No one wakes up and says, "When I grow up I'm going to be an exotic dancer named Soleil." Instead, they say, "I'm going to be a star." For Skylar Lynn, she always dreamed of being a star. From the time she could talk, the words "movie" and "star" were coming out of her mouth with every sentence. She never in her wildest dreams thought she would be playing the role of a star by being an exotic dancer. The thought of being labeled a "stripper" never crossed her mind until she was scraping by on nothing, working three jobs to stay afloat, and living in a rundown New York City studio that looked like a Hell's Kitchen efficiency.

Skylar was still trying to wake up to reality and really feel the whole entire role as the exotic dancer. The light began to shine from the broken glass right into her thoughts as a flashback from her days in the *Playground of Dreams* began to come into her vision.

EARLIER YEARS

It was her days playing dress up as a star in her *Playground of Dreams* that calmed the storm brewing in her Midwestern home. Skylar grew up in a typical middle-class family, but looking through a magnifying lens, you could see many cracks. Her vision for her dreams became foggy as the sound of thunder in her home began to get louder. Inside her home life things were starting to break apart: a lost marriage between her parents, a mom who suffered bouts of depression, an overworked father, and constant chaos among her siblings. The stage of a broken home began to fade any hope of lightness into darkness as her *Playground of Dreams* started to fade into a gloomy setting.

However, it was when she brought herself to plug into her *Playground of Dreams* that those visions of being a star allowed her to jump, skip, and hop over the cracked glass in her broken home, especially during Halloween.

Halloween was her chance to dress up as a star once a year. It was during this time she truly felt like one, stepping out of character and into a dream. Each Halloween gave Skylar the opportunity to capture the goddess qualities of a star she had watched in both TV and film growing up. Some of these goddess-like costumes and characters she played each Halloween were The Little Mermaid, Spiderwoman, Artemis, Queen of Hearts, and Strawberry Shortcake. These characters allowed her inner goddess to glow as she began to feel the warmth of *The Silver Lights*.

Skylar had no clue that her biggest performance was awaiting her in the role of Soleil, the exotic dancer. It would be this controversial role that would give Skylar the chance write her first screenplay, *The City of Dreams*, but first Skylar would have master the role of the understudy by embracing Strip Club 101.

The countdown towards Skylar's first days at Silver Lights were approaching. How would a naive girl from the Midwest go from just another extra behind the scenes to landing a leading role, center stage in *The City of Dreams*? The answer lay in mastering the role of an understudy, and with that came observing, studying, and getting familiar with the world of stripping.

THE STORY OF SKYLAR LYNN
IN *THE CITY OF DREAMS* CONTINUES

For Skylar Lynn, her new role as an exotic dancer rescued her character from sinking to nothing in *The City of Dreams*. You can see her character come back to life in her new role as Soleil. It gave her voice the strength to break free from her inner monologue. It was the power of her new character's voice that allowed her to walk over the pieces of broken glass, which represented broken parts of her soul. With no more broken glass in sight, she finally felt free to soar. For the first time in fifteen years, she could finally see past her broken spirit as the light of silver began to touch her spirit, faithfully guiding her into the night as she awaited one more day to leave behind a life of slippers in exchange for a life of silver heels.

ACT IV, SCENE 2
THE MAKING OF A STAR

INTERIOR: PENTHOUSE CLUB

FADE IN

Skylar nervously walked into the Penthouse, another popular New York City gentlemen's club with her gay best friend, Javier. She and Javier had met in the real estate office in her first year as an agent. He had been born in Brazil but moved to the United States with his family when he was five. Javier looked like a carbon copy of Ricky Martin but with no accent. He was known as the schmoozer in the office and had a reputation in real estate that he would literally do just about anything within legal boundaries to close a deal. He loved the excitement of going out in NYC and saw any social outing as a potential for a sale.

Skylar told Javier in confidence about her new role at Silver Lights and trusted he would not say anything to anyone in the office. In passing, he would always joke with her that becoming a stripper would save her financial status. He would say to her, "If God made me a woman, I would use it to win over all the hot men and real estate deals." Skylar would brush off his jokes because the idea of becoming a stripper seemed so out of left field, but at the same time her financial issues were starting to weaken any visions for becoming a star in The City of Dreams.

When Skylar told Javier about her audition and her start date, he was so excited that you'd think he had just gotten hired at Silver Lights. Right away, he suggested Skylar check out Silver Lights' biggest competitor, Penthouse, which was right down the street.

As the two entered Penthouse, you can see the ambience of the red decor everywhere, from the drapery to the lights. The door guy Charlie, a friend of Javier's, greeted him with a friendly gesture and hug.

DIALOGUE

CHARLIE: Hey, stranger, it's been a long time? What have you been up to?

JAVIER: Hey, Charlie, it's good to see you. I have been tied down to my cubicle. It's been crazy busy with new customers and listings.

CHARLIE: Busy is good. (*He looks at Javier and then gestures at Skylar.*) Who is this? You never told me you had such a beautiful friend.

JAVIER: This is my close friend, Skylar. We work together in real estate, and she is new to the language of stripping. If you get my drift.

SKYLAR: Hi, pleasure to meet you. This is my second time in a strip club.

CHARLIE: Really? Why? You're missing out on a lot of great drink specials, and drama!

SKYLAR: Drama and drink specials. I do feel I have been missing out. Who doesn't love a good drink and a good drama, and you can get the real thing instead of watching it at home on Netflix. I'm in!

CHARLIE: You can always stop in and take a look. I'm here outside part of the time and in the back office in the day time. So you never really answered my question: why is this your second time at a strip club?

SKYLAR: No reason in particular. I just never had the desire or need until now.

CHARLIE: So your curiosity has been piqued, and now you have one foot in the door and one foot out. Are you going to be the girl who gets out just as quick as they get in, or are you going to be the girl that stays in? No need to say. I already know.

SKYLAR: I'm staying.

CHARLIE: That is a great decision, and Javier would agree, too.

JAVIER: I think it's the best decision.

CHARLIE. He may not look like it, but he is a strip club expert. (Smiles at Javier, then points towards the inside entrance.) You can go through there and straight through the glass doors. Enjoy.

JAVIER: Now, don't be giving her any ideas now.

Skylar and Javier walk through the doors. Skylar is still in shock from the conversation between Charlie and Javier, and that she referred to Javier as "a strip club expert."

Javier and Skylar go to take a seat at the side bar, which is positioned to the left side of the center stage. The bartender seems to know him, and a few dancers from afar do, too. It's quite obvious that Javier is a regular customer.

A bartender by the name of Rachel with a thick Long Island accent warmly greets Javier.

RACHEL: Captain and Coke?

JAVIER: You know me too well. This is my friend Skylar. She works with me in real estate.

RACHEL: Nice to meet you. Any friend of Javier's is a friend of mine. What can I get you?

SKYLAR: What type of energy drinks do you have?

RACHEL: We have Red Bull, monster, and a new organic energy drink that was just put out called Zen Energy.

SKYLAR: That sounds interesting. I will try that.

RACHEL: This round is on the house since it's your first night here.

Rachel serves the drinks as the DJ begins to transition dance songs, and then a new dancer by the name of Barbie goes on center stage to perform. *Barbie, a statuesque blonde no older than thirty, starts twirling around the pole and gyrating her hips as the tempo of the music begins to slow. Javier gives Skylar the low down of the club and what to expect. He gestures towards Barbie.*

JAVIER: See how Barbie is dancing to the beats of the music, making eye contact with the customers, and adding her own personality to the routine?

SKYLAR: Personality to the routine? It's just pole dancing naked.

JAVIER: Girl, it's not just pole dancing naked! You have to start thinking of your dance performance as the performance to your dreams. The more you pour your heart and soul into each performance by connecting with the music, audience, and yourself, the more you are going to shine like a star.

SKYLAR: I'm a star.

JAVIER: Yes, you are. You need to think of yourself as a star every time you get up on that stage. So now that you actually took the plunge to become a dancer, I do a have a confession to make.

SKYLAR: What is it?

JAVIER: My mom was a stripper for fifteen years when we first moved to this country.

SKYLAR: She was?

JAVIER: Yes, and I didn't find out until the age of nine, when she was having an argument with my dad about the club.

SKYLAR: Wow. I never would have thought in a million years that Mrs. Gonzalez, the Spanish Betty Crocker, at one point was an exotic dancer.

JAVIER: Exotic dancers are mothers, students, entrepreneurs, and everyday women that are just striving for more. There is no particular profile of an exotic dancer. The media creates the profile of a stripper by feeding the public propaganda and lies to sell stories. Dancing has so many types of women from all areas of life. Without dancing, my mom would have never been a star for us. She provided us with food, clothes, a safe home, and education. I respect the women that do this because it's not easy to work in an industry that has more negatives working against you than positives.

SKYLAR: (Shocked) I don't even know where to begin. All those jokes of me becoming a stripper to ease my finances make complete sense.

JAVIER: I was only trying to help you, because I knew that dancing would alleviate some of the financial burdens.

SKYLAR: I love how you referred to your mom as a star. I'm going to remember that as I start tomorrow. When I get nervous, I'm going close my eyes and tell myself "I'm a star."

JAVIER: Good, because you are one, and baby, I got your back—always. Like I said, if I was sexy woman in this lifetime, I would jump at being a stripper in a heartbeat!

Javier turns towards the stage and sees Barbie walking towards him. He turns towards Skylar to make the introduction.

JAVIER: Barbie is a good friend of mine. She has been in the business for a little over five years and goes to school during the day, finishing her bachelor's in political science. If you have any questions, she is the one to ask.

Barbie, whose real name is Ava Marie, comes over to the bar area, waving to Javier. She is from South Carolina and has the looks of a super model and mannerisms that classify her as a southern belle the moment she says, "Hey." No one would ever assume if they saw her outside the club, that this conservative-looking lady would be working as a stripper.

BARBIE: Hey, y'all.

JAVIER: So good to see you. (*Gives her a hug.*) Barbie, this is my close friend Skylar. She works with me in real estate.

BARBIE: Hi, it's a pleasure to meet you darling. What brings you out with this wild one? (*Giggles.*)

SKYLAR: (*Nervously*) I wanted to check out this club because I just got hired at Silver Lights.

BARBIE: Silver Lights, really? We are in competition with Silver Lights. (*She looks at Javier.*)

SKYLAR: Javier did mention that it's a competitor. I just wanted to get a better feeling of the industry before my first day.

JAVIER: I thought this would be the perfect introduction before she is thrown to the wolves tomorrow.

BARBIE: Javier, I was the same way, too. I was clueless to what dancing was about. I thought it was just about looking beautiful and even being slutty! (*Giggles.*)

SKYLAR: Slutty?

BARBIE: Yes, don't get scared off by the reputation that all dancers are slutty because, in fact, that's not the case. It's more about selling the experience, from the conversation to the exotic dances to the more intimate dances in the champagne rooms.

SKYLAR: Intimate conversations in the champagne rooms?

BARBIE: Angel, don't look so scared. I can reassure you it's not exactly what it appears in the movies. It's been a blessing.

There is something so beautiful and raw when you become open to the idea of dancing naked in front of others. Like you, I was clueless when I came to the world of exotic entertainment and had to depend on listening to the rhythm of the music to connect with my mind, body, and spirit.

SKYLAR: Music, dancing, and being naked have a lot of spiritual elements, especially when you combine all three.

BARBIE: The way you view yourself as an exotic dancer will determine how successful you will be. When is your start date?

SKYLAR: (*Nervously*) Tomorrow.

BARBIE: Have you met Tony yet? He is the general manager over there.

SKYLAR: Redmond is.

BARBIE: I have known Redmond forever. We are from the same hometown. He is second to Tony. Tony is the one who heads all operations. You can't miss him—he looks like Mr. Clean. He comes in on weekends and pops in during the nighttime, usually Wednesdays and Thursdays.

The tone of "I have known Redmond forever" implied the two were more than casual acquaintances. The two at some point had been an item, whether it be in high school or at the club. The way Barbie was talking made Skylar think something went down that left Barbie with no choice but to go work for their competitor, Penthouse, even with Redmond up for a big promotion.

The first moment Skylar saw Redmond at the club, she had gotten butterflies in her stomach. She had strong feelings the moment she set eyes on him, without even knowing him. The way her heart skipped a beat, the sweat in between her eyebrows, the way she lost her words when in his presence. She had felt a soul connection with him and wondered if he had felt it too. He did notice something was off with the way he felt when he first met her, but he couldn't pin it down. His mind was more distracted with the daily pressures of sales and management issues, over discovering where and in what lifetime did his soul recognize Skylar's.

SKYLAR: Did you go to high school together?

BARBIE: Not exactly. Our families are friends through business, but I don't want to get into it. Everything is cool with us.

SKYLAR: Ok.

JAVIER: Sky, if you have any more questions, you should get Barbie's digits.

The two exchange numbers.

SKYLAR: *(She turns to Barbie.)* By the way, how did you get into this industry?

BARBIE: Well, Sky. I truly never imagined I would end up an exotic dancer, but the dominoes didn't fall exactly the way I had planned.

SKYLAR: How so?

BARBIE: I was a beauty queen in my small town with dreams of pursuing modeling with a big agency and getting a career in fashion design. Shortly after I moved to the Big Apple, the modeling jobs were slim to none, and if I got a job it was only enough to pay for groceries. I didn't realize that with so many beautiful models in this city the odds were against me, so one day when bills were piling up and I was worried about eviction, I was scouring the advertisements and there was one that Silver Lights had placed, and at the time it just seemed right. And you know what, Sky? It was the best decision of my life. I am about to graduate college, and I'm pursuing a law degree upon my acceptance to NYU next year.

SKYLAR: That's amazing to hear. Can I ask you something?

BARBIE: Sure.

SKYLAR: Would you become a dancer all over again if you didn't need to?

BARBIE: I would because dancing, especially the element of the pole and being topless, is something that has given me a newfound freedom as a woman that I never knew existed. I feel more confident and in touch with my inner goddess, my feminine side.

JAVIER: I hope Barbie's story has inspired you. (*Looks at Sky*)

BARBIE: Sky, if you do have any questions relating to champagne rooms, lap dancing, pole dancing, or something that is not sitting right, please reach out.

SKYLAR: Thanks, guys. I still have a knot in my stomach about tomorrow, though.

BARBIE: You're going to be fine. Don't look too much into the dancing topless part. Instead, view it as your dancing your way to becoming a star.

SKYLAR: I can take that.

FADE OUT

Skylar's little adventure to Penthouse with Javier left her exploring her understudy role further. She was thinking of her new role and why Barbie left Silver Lights if she had such a great experience, especially for a second-rate club like Penthouse.

She wondered if the real reason Barbie left Silver Lights was because of a breakup, or did it have to do with politics? Skylar really had no clue, or could it be that the story of Barbie is something only seen on drama-filled TV shows, where she is working for both clubs, one as "spy" for Silver Lights to get insider information for their future merger. This way Steven Banks would shy away from the Penthouse deal and automatically go with franchising Silver Lights.

Steven Banks was the king of hospitality in New York City. The New York Post had run an article six months ago about his new promotion to Gemstone Hospitality and his departure form City Group. The article stated that he was in charge of allocating a fifteen-million-dollar investment between two different industries: one of them was the world of adult entertainment, gentlemen's club establishments, or the world of fast food. Would Steven give part of the funds to making Silver Lights a national franchise, or go with its competitor Penthouse, giving it a new facelift in terms of marketing and making it a members-only club for the elite? Skylar's ears weren't deaf to the rumors as she religiously read up on Page Six weekly. Since she was in the role of the understudy before her first day, she did make herself aware of any drama boiling so she wouldn't be caught in the heat of her future scenes in The City of Dreams.

ACT IV, SCENE 3
THE #6 SUBWAY RIDE HOME

FADE IN

The story of *The Silver Lights* guiding Skylar towards starring in her debut, *The City of Dreams*, continues as she exits Penthouse. After she hugs Javier, they part ways. She takes the number six subway all the way back to her rundown apartment. The subway ride home seemed more like the Twilight Zone. Everything she had envisioned when she moved to *The City of Dreams* had spilled down the gutter at the sound of the broken glass. The late night crowd on the subway seemed blurry, and all that made sense to Skylar was the recurring *Silver Lights* that came into her vision as she got deeper into her trance. The sound of the "ninety-sixth street exit" blared over the intercom, startling Skylar from her visions of *The Silver Lights* guiding her as she woke up to exit the train.

For some reason, during the walk back to her apartment, she felt differently than she had on her usual walks through the cold streets of New York City. She no longer felt the hardness of the pavement or the wind chill as she walked home. The streets from *The City of Dreams* seemed to feel lighter, and brighter. You can see the reflection of light begin to fill her scenes with faith, elevating her spirit towards the power of now, before she enters her apartment, and begins to reflect on moving towards the light.

DIALOGUE

SKYLAR: Thank you higher power for showing me the way. I am starting to feel your warm presence guiding me out of this struggle. I feel your light every time I walk in darkness. I feel your magnetic force pulling me towards the spotlight. Most importantly, I feel and see faith shining down upon me in my scenes as I leave the broken glass behind to make way for my starring role in *The City of Dreams*.

FADE OUT

CHAPTER 7
THE STAGE OF DREAMS

The Silver Lights began to spotlight the small-town girl's spirit behind the scenes as her shadows of doubt began to fade away. As the hours dwindled down, you could see a leading lady waiting silently backstage for her day to shine as the warm feeling from *The Silver Lights* began to guide the small-town girl, step by step into dancing her way towards her Hollywood Dream.

ACT V, SCENE 1
DAY 1 AS A STRIPPER

INT: BACKSTAGE DRESSING ROOM

FADE IN

The dressing room in the club this time didn't feel strange, but rather comfortable. Although this was only her second time walking through the 70s-inspired art deco dressing room, she felt more relaxed. The dressing room began to comfort her new character Soleil so much that she saw her visions from The Playground of Dreams come back to life. The words "Can I?" "Should I?" or "I can't" were no longer part of her dialogue, instead the words "I am a star" were resonating in her new dialogue.

She checked in with House Mom Shay and was given a locker where she was to put her belongings each night. She was told once she finished her makeup, hair, and wardrobe, she was to go see Tony, head of operations. Every new dancer was required to go through a quick orientation with Tony, a veteran of the club business and a former male dancer. His thick Brooklyn accent and his Arnold Schwarzenegger body gave him the nickname "The Lion King" at Silver Lights.

Skylar proceeded to transform into her new character by stripping down to nothing. She started to get into her character Soleil by slipping into the risqué red teddy dress that she had bought at the Hustler Store. She began to do her makeup as if she was turning into a goddess.

Skylar loved to play with makeup when she had dates, events, or something special. Typically, she just wore basic cover-up, a light bronzer during the day, lip gloss, and mascara. Her everyday makeup was natural and not heavy. Skylar truly loved playing with makeup and creating different looks. The look she was hoping to achieve for her first day was a 1920s pin-up girl. She started to prep her face with foundation, and then contour strategically like Kim K and all her favorites. She then accentuated her full lips with a rose berry lipstick and a nude gloss. She began to make her lips "juicy" and her eyes mesmerizing as her new character Soleil came alive.

Once she completed her look from head to toe, she gazed into the mirror. She felt the warmth of her new character for the first time as she opened up her spirit to the reflection of "sunshine" she saw in the mirror. This feeling she felt was indescribable. It was the closest she felt to bliss as The Silver Lights once again came beaming down with faith, shining the warmest light upon her childhood gift, so leaving her slippers behind in The City of Dreams in exchange for a life of Silver Heels would elevate her talent to dance her way to the top in her second feature, Hollywood Dreams.

Since becoming part of Silver Lights, she finally felt like she was given a second chance to become a star, playing a real character who danced into a spotlight of dreams. Her lines were no longer scripted and directed, but improvised and read with hope, giving her one last chance to outshine her bleak forecast. Her aura became lighter, *brighter, and more captivating as she set her visions towards The Stage of Dreams.*

FADE OUT

ACT V, SCENE 2
STRIPPER ORIENTATION

INT: BACK BAR

ORIENTATION AT THE RESTAURANT BAR

FADE IN

After checking in with House Mom Shay, Skylar headed out towards the back bar area where the steakhouse was attached to the club. She was greeted by perhaps one of the most charismatic characters at Silver Lights, Tony Murano, also known as "Tee," who was an industry leader in the world of exotic dancing. He had contacts worldwide in the business and was the best at turning around poorly performing clubs and making them profitable. If there was a problem, Tony was the first to know, and roar, about it! If revenue wasn't meeting monthly numbers, Tony was the guy who roared a solution, and if there was legal drama, Tony was the first to put the lid on it! No wonder Tony was recognized all over the industry as the legend in the world of stripping.

DIALOGUE

Tony's inviting personality made Skylar Lynn feel comfortable as he pulled out the chair from under the table.

TONY: Take a seat here, Skylar, or should I call you "Soleil"?

SKYLAR: Call me Soleil.

TONY: Soleil, it's a pleasure to meet you. I'm excited to have you as part of our family here at Silver Lights. Can I get you a drink?

SKYLAR: Sure. I will take the new energy drink called "ZEN"?

TONY: Hey Liv, can you get me one Jack and ginger, and the new energy drink called "ZEN"? Sounds like something from a Buddhist temple.

SKYLAR: (*Laughs*) It's made of Asian ingredients that are natural for an energy drink.

TONY: Interesting.

LIV: Coming right up.

TONY: As I was saying, we are one big, happy family at Silver Lights, Soleil. (*Pauses.*) When the family starts to become broken, that's where I come in and make sure it's still one. Understood?

SKYLAR: Yes, sir.

TONY: Call me Tee.

SKYLAR: Yes, Tee.

TONY: I am the first person you see if there are any major problems. The second person you see if you have minor issues like conflicts with dancers, customers, or getting paid is Redmond.

SKYLAR: Can you go over the VIP rooms?

TONY: I was just about to get to that. Are you a mind reader?

SKYLAR: Some say I am. (*Smiles*)

TONY: Well, maybe we have you have in the wrong position. (*Chuckles.*) We should put you in finance . . .

SKYLAR: Been there, done that.

TONY: You didn't like it?

SKYLAR: I'm here wearing this sexy number, so let's say I was far from employee of the year. I got burnt out being on autopilot, so here I am hoping to change my story of a starving artist.

TONY: Soleil, do you trust me?

SKYLAR: I guess I can trust you. I mean I just met you. (*Chuckles.*)

TONY: Hear me out, Soleil. Sliver Lights can be a spotlight to your dreams, so you can change your story. Many girls such as yourself find themselves here as their last hope. You hear what I'm saying?

SKYLAR: Yes, I do.

TONY: If you play your cards right, it can be your new dream. Oh yeah, I forgot to mention we had Steven Tyler from Aerosmith last week and New York's biggest social media and business influencer, Jake Ryan, walk through the doors.

SKYLAR: Jake Ryan. He is Instagram and YouTube famous.

TONY: This is just the beginning. You have no idea the power, prestige, and influence you will find each night. So getting to the most important part, now I want to discuss the champagne rooms, the bread and butter of Silver Lights. The way the champagne rooms operate, since you are new, is once there is interest from a customer who wants to spend private time with you or a group of dancers, you then take them to Michael Donahue, Senior Host, or Frankie Martinez, second in charge of champagne rooms. If they are not found, then you look for Redmond. They will talk about pricing, specifics, and run their card without you ever having to discuss numbers and champagne rooms in the same sentence. Remember, never discuss prices for rooms—that's the management's job, so avoid it at all costs.

SKYLAR: That's good to know.

TONY: You never discuss price directly. That's where the hosts come in and seal the deal to discuss numbers. Just take the customer by the hand once they are interested to the host and let them handle it from there. As you get more comfortable selling champagne rooms and doing them, it will become automatic. I'm going to partner you up with Lola for the week. She has a stellar reputation here at Silver Lights for being the premiere dancer of the year, and for selling the most rooms and bottles for the club in 2014. She has been with the club for five years. I will introduce her to you shortly. Is this all making sense?

SKYLAR: Yeah, it is.

TONY: Guess what, I have some good news?

SKYLAR: What?

TONY: At Silver Lights, we reward you when you are making money for the club. The more champagne bottles you sell, the more money you are going to get in your weekly paycheck. The paychecks are run through Dance Dollars at the club, which also tracks every time a bottle is sold in the POS system. At the end of the month, we total all the dancers' sales of champagne bottles and rooms, and the two dancers with the highest sales get a fifteen-hundred-dollar bonus for the month on top of their Dance Dollars. It's a great incentive on top of the dances to really push the champagne rooms and bottles.

SKYLAR: (nervously) Push the champagne rooms . . .

TONY: You look nervous. Trust me, I have your back. I will tell you a little secret. In another lifetime, about fifteen years ago, I was a male dancer—that helped me escape a life of crime. I'm grateful every day for this industry because it saved me from a prison sentence, a life of smuggling drugs and laundering money, and digging my own grave.

SKYLAR: (*stunned*) Really?

TONY: It's true. You can look at this position two ways: a meal ticket, or a role of a lifetime.

SKYLAR: How do you know that I am not looking at this as a role of a lifetime?

TONY: I didn't make an assumption. I'm just telling you what I have seen over the past ten years; either you can get swallowed up and then spit back out on the cold streets, or you can make a name for yourself. Remember to erase any stereotypes you have seen about strip clubs from films like *Striptease*, *The Sopranos*, or *Showgirls* because behind every drama-filled story, there is light.

SKYLAR: I love *Sopranos* though. It would be exciting if there was some drama going on that mirrored a bit of the show. I need some real life mafia material for my future screenplay, *Hollywood Dreams*.

TONY: Baby girl, I grew up on the streets with the Marziano Family. Do you know who they are?

SKYLAR: No. Are they part of Bertolli family food empire?

TONY: Not exactly. Google the Marzianos when you get a chance. We did have one of the executives from the Bertolli family in here last week. They are big spenders, and they love blondes! In about three months you will have racy stories, interesting characters, and drama for your next feature, *Hollywood Dreams* . . .

SKYLAR: My dream is to be bigger than the next Carrie Bradshaw from *Sex and the City.*

TONY: I like the way you're talking, so you have some big *Silver Heels* to fill now.

SKYLAR: I do.

(*Tony looks down at his phone.*)

TONY: Soleil, I'm getting an important text from Steven Banks of Gemstone Hospitality. This could be huge in our future expansion of franchising the Silver Lights brand. One more thing, please check in with the DJ Pauly after this. They will also be calling you to stage twice a night unless you sell a champagne room. I just got word from DJ Pauly that your first performance will be in twenty minutes. After you finish, I'm going to introduce you to Lola.

SKYLAR: Great, I can't wait.

TONY: Just remember, Soleil, you are a star.

FADE OUT

The countdown was ticking away until Skylar would make her debut on the Stage of Dreams. It was a matter of minutes before Skylar Lynn would forever be turning her back on her shadow for something lighter and brighter. Skylar would have two songs to make it rain. You can see the sweat from her brow disappear, the burning fear in her eyes dim, and the forced smile become effortless. The warmer colors begin to penetrate Skylar's aura as the reflection of The Silver Lights begin to guide her faithfully beyond the Stage of Dreams, and in the direction of her Hollywood Dreams.

CHAPTER 8
HOLLYWOOD DREAMS

The Hollywood Dream starts the moment we open our eyes and ears to the "magic" of film. The universal language that film gives each one of us on a subconscious level creates a larger pathway of hope and inspiration. The stories from the big screen that touch our soul, captivate our thoughts, and awaken our dreams are the ones that bring us closer to the power of *The Silver Lights*. For Skylar, her dreams of being a Hollywood screenwriter and actress were awakened even more from the moment she slipped into her first pair of *Silver Heels*. You can see the way the *Silver Heels* give her the strength to perform with elegance. As Skylar waits patiently backstage, the magic of the *Silver Heels* elevate her feet to connect her mind, body, and spirit, as minutes are dwindling down for her first dance performance.

DJ Pauly was down to the last song set before Skylar's performance. *The Silver Lights* once again entered her picture, this time flashing the song and dance "Greased Lightning" from one of her favorite dance movies, *Grease*.

Skylar immediately was taken back to this scene for a few seconds and the picture of John Travolta and the male cast performing this song ignited a fire of passion.

Would Skylar Lynn be able to perform like her favorite dance stars, John Travolta and Olivia Newton-John from the movie *Grease*, or would she just freeze up on stage? These questions were building up behind the scenes as minutes were ticking down to seconds, and soon the small-town girl from the Midwest would never be the same again as she took the stage to rock n' roll.

ACT V, SCENE 3
ROCK N' ROLL

INT: DJ BOOTH

FADE IN

DJ Pauly, a former punk rock musician from the late 90s. His face resembled Eddie Van Halen's. He was still trying to live his days of partying like a rock star through his DJ position at Silver Lights. His demeanor was uplifting, comedic, and supportive when it came to announcing the exotic dancers and running the music production.

DJ PAULY: Soleil, I'm Pauly. Pleasure to meet you. I heard you are from the Midwest.

SKYLAR: Yes, I'm from Cleveland.

DJ PAULY: I was there in the late 90s performing with a Van Halen cover band.

SOLEIL: Got to love Van Halen, but I prefer Aerosmith.

DJ PAULY: Aerosmith? You're definitely on my shit list. Just kidding.

SKYLAR: Oh, geez.

DJ PAULY: What type of music do you like to dance to?

SKYLAR: I love rock n' roll, Aerosmith obviously. (*Smiles.*) I also like pop too, like Beyoncé.

DJ PAULY: Nice. I know what I'm going to play for you. The first song will be rock n' roll, and the second song will be pop. Just stand over there, and when I announce your name, walk towards center stage. Remember you are going to be on stage for two songs, performing only on the center stage. During the weekends, it's three-song sets using all stages. You have less than a minute until I announce your name. Remember to have fun, and don't forget to rock n' roll!

SKYLAR: Any tips for virgins?

DJ PAULY: Skylar. I'm a man of rock n' roll. I love groupies, so you can't go that route with me.

SKYLAR: I meant to say first-timers.

DJ PAULY: Better word choice.

SKYLAR: Ha ha.

DJ PAULY: You're starting to grow on me. I do prefer girls with tattoos, but I like your humor. Remember to feel the music, connect with the audience, and rock n' roll with the pole!

SKYLAR: Rock n' roll. I really like that.

DJ PAULY: Remember, song one, the top can be on and song two, the top must come off. Most dancers take their top off halfway into song one.

Skylar nodded and could feel the knots in her stomach becoming tighter, her mouth becoming drier, and her sweat perspiring under her armpits as her whole body began to quiver. Her nerves were starting to get the best of her. DJ Pauly over the intercom says, "Tonight, for her first time ever in Silver Lights, the sexy Soleil makes her debut."

The moment Skylar heard the name "Soleil" announced over the intercom, The Silver Lights began to flash visions from her Playground of Dreams. It was these lights that connected her third eye to her future visions of her dancing the night away at The Golden Globes.

Who would have ever guessed that a young woman from the Midwest by the name of Skylar Lynn would be given a chance to dance her way to the top of The City of Dreams and into an award-winning role that would later spotlight her gift to writing her Hollywood Dream?

The Silver Lights that kept on flashing in and out of Skylar's scenes all throughout The City of Dreams was a sign from the universe that Skylar was destined for bigger and better things and that her dance routine would be more than a striptease.

All of sudden, over the intercom DJ Pauly announced "Soleil" signaling her to the center stage. She took one last deep breath, and as she exhaled she began to pray to the heavens above to give her strength, humility, and grace to give the performance of a lifetime in her first night at Silver Lights.

FADE OUT

ACT V, SCENE 4
WHERE DREAMS ARE MADE OF

INT: CENTER STAGE

FADE IN

The music began to play as the first song shifted into the lyrics of the chorus. As the beats got stronger, The Silver Lights began to shine on stage. Her entire body from head to toe began to feel the warmth of The Silver Lights as her spirit felt the vibration of the music. Her eyes became lighter, her body became lithe, and her face became enchanting with each beat of music. She began to attempt to twirl around the pole, moving her hips sensually and gyrating with the music. With each beat, she began to embrace the vibrations of the music as her body got closer to the silver pole. With her back parallel to the pole and her face to the audience, she began to feel the uplifting energy of the music, moving her hips erotically down the pole, inch by inch. She seductively began to kneel on the ground, still shaking her hips and booty to the rhythm of the music, and just like that, all of a sudden, the music changed again, and the DJ's words "rock n' roll" came into her mind right before she was about to remove the top portion of her dress.

As she removed the top part of her dress, there was a slight ounce of hesitation that came into play for just a millisecond, but it went away as The Silver Lights came into her vision. She began to move her dress down her body until all you could see was her boobs and part of her dress taking on the shape of a skirt. Regardless of the fact she was semi-nude in front of strangers, the feelings of darkness began to become lighter as she became topless. The moment she embraced being semi-nude to the audience was the same time she experienced a euphoric freedom that left her feeling more liberated than she could have ever imagined. She felt like a rock star living her dreams.

The music switched beats again in the second song, and she began to focus on the music within, rather than outside. As she focused within, The Silver Lights began to shine faith over her Playground of Dreams, spotlighting a new direction away from the shattered glass. The shattered glass in The City of Dreams was no longer in front of her Hollywood Dreams, but behind.

She began to dance her way up slowly from the floor to a standing position. Her body became parallel to the pole as she continued to dance with the music. You can see as she danced with the music, The Silver Lights beamed against the silver pole.

The silver pole was more than just a fixture as Soleil wrapped one foot around the pole, seductively shaking her hips with the music, and placing her left hand on one hip, while the right hand grabbed the pole. Then, as she moved her hips with the music, her left leg swung around the silver pole as her left hand from her hip moved through her long, honey-blonde hair, tossing it back. The beats of music continued to pick up as she made one last dance sequence twirling around the silver pole, getting down to nothing except a G-string.

She remembered to connect with her audience while dancing, making eye contact directly with some of them. In one corner, there was a group of Wall Street men in the VIP section mixed in with dancers, and in another corner there was a group of patrons conversing with more dancers, and from afar in the bar area, Skylar saw Tony and Redmond watching her performance.

As she continued to dance topless with less than a minute remaining, the fog in her eyes cleared up, the storm on her face disappeared, and the character of a starving artist became full.

FADE OUT

FADE IN

Redmond, a country boy from rural South Carolina, moved to *The City of Dreams* in pursuit of landing his leading role of being the next Leo DiCaprio. Unfortunately, *The City of Dreams* didn't have an opening for the next Leo, and for Redmond his leading role of stardom happened to take a back seat. He learned quickly he didn't have the skills to be on center stage, so he gracefully accepted his role as a barback, working his way up over the next five years to being cast as the Assistant Manager at Silver Lights.

His story mirrored Skylar's in that both were from small towns and moved to *The City of Dreams* with hopes of landing their starring roles. However, shortly after arriving, Redmond, like Skylar, saw the direction of his *Hollywood Dreams* crashing. His day job of being a struggling actor was not footing any of his bills, and his character in *The City of Dreams* was dying off because he couldn't find a role that suited him.

His high school sweetheart, Ava Marie, referred to as Barbie in the club because of her beautiful blonde looks and hourglass figure, had moved to *The City of Dreams* with him to pursue modeling and a career in fashion.

Two months into their move, they both came to realize their dreams were drowning in *The City of Dreams* rather than soaring. Terrified at the thought of going back to the rural south, they both had to find new roles that would allow their characters to do more than just float.

Ava got hired with Silver Lights and the rest was history, while on the other hand, a month passed by, and Redmond was still sinking further into his disappointment. Ava suggested he work at Silver Lights, and she would talk to Tony about getting him a job as a barback. The next day, after talking to Tony, Redmond was called in for an interview and was hired on the spot. Little did Redmond know that five years later, his role of barback would soon lead him to being second in charge of the biggest strip club in all of New York City, and the possibility of becoming part owner if the merger of Gemstone Hospitality came through.

THE DRAMA BEGINS

Fast forward five years later, Ava Marie left *Silver Lights*, just three months after rumors were starting to spread that her beau Redmond had hooked up after hours with porn star Amber Shay in the Howard Stern champagne room. He defended his character by stating the malicious rumors were spread to create drama as he had had a falling out with Pierre Lucca. Supposedly, Pierre Lucca was crossing a boundary with Ava Marie, not just in the champagne rooms but outside the club, too, pursuing her to break up with Redmond and move into his penthouse in the Wall Street area.

Barbie really had no proof except for the whispers she was hearing from other dancers. Within every rumor, Barbie knew there was part truth and part lie. Someone was obviously telling the truth and the other was lying. Either Redmond had an affair with Amber Shay in the Howard Stern champagne room, or Pierre Lucca made up a rumor to make his ego feel better about being rejected, so he could end up winning Barbie over. Someone here was at fault, but Barbie, being the loyal southern belle, decided to believe Redmond and cut ties with Pierre Luca.

The real problem lay in Redmond's job responsibilities. He was the first person all the weekly porn stars or adult features communicated with from Silver Lights. He was the front man dealing with booking, marketing, and handling the weekly adult stars who would perform at Silver Lights. The drama of her boyfriend sleeping with a porn star spun so out of control that one day she walked into Tony's office in a complete meltdown and just quit. Barbie couldn't take coming to work and hearing the rumors and gossip every day among other dancers, so she left Silver Lights, but in reality she really never left.

Before leaving, Tony had made Barbie an offer she couldn't resist, that she would still get paid from Silver Lights as an employee over an independent contractor for working one day a week in the office. This position was made up for her real job as an undercover spy at

Penthouse. This way it worked out to her advantage; she was not only getting a salary as an employee but also tips and Dance Dollars for being a feature entertainer at Penthouse. This conspiracy was only known between Redmond, Tony, and herself. They swore to never to leak this to anyone, no matter what. The code word for them to discuss this weekly was "dirty martini specials."

If this conspiracy leaked out to anyone, all three of them could be facing jail time for corporate espionage, not to mention forgoing a multi-million-dollar investment from Gemstone Hospitality that could possibly turn Silver Lights into the largest strip club franchise ever. Rumors had it there was a big drug ring going on behind the scenes of Penthouse that was enticing high rollers and some of their biggest Wall Street customers like Sapphire Investments and Onyx Equities to be spending more time over there lately. If Barbie could get her hands on hard evidence concerning drug racketeering while being undercover at Penthouse, this could be a big break for Silver Lights to becoming a nationwide franchise. Penthouse would completely go under for drug racketeering, leaving Gemstone Hospitality no choice but to invest in Silver Lights.

Barbie was faced with this lucrative opportunity working as an undercover spy and exotic dancer, so she felt she had no choice but to forgive and forget the rumors of Redmond having sex with Amber Shay, or else she would risk losing her dreams of attending law school by putting herself in a position that would leave her nowhere to dance in New York City. She would have to work out of state, where her future acceptance to NYU would be put on hold, and she would have to take out loans.

Deep down inside, she felt betrayed, harboring anger towards Redmond. The two no longer made frequent love, and their everyday encounters were minimal exchanges of small talk as they used to do everything together from cooking, watching TV, working out, and getting coffee before work. Their relationship was already somewhat cracked, but it was on its way to tearing apart. The Claddagh rings, an Irish love ring that they had given each other before moving to *The City of Dreams*, was gone as Ava had tossed hers out the window and his in the garbage after she heard about the rumors. The longer that Ava held on to this resentment, the more likely that Redmond would bail from their relationship and end up finding a real after-hours girlfriend to play with.

Redmond was a ladies' man with his southern charm, devilishly handsome looks, and piercing blue eyes that just caught you off guard. He had a line of dancers just waiting to play with him when the club closed down. Most of the dancers during orientation couldn't help but get butterflies as his muscles popped out from his dress suit, and the whiff of his cologne was laced with pheromones. There were about eight crushes from dancers he had hired, and it was pretty obvious it was like a puppy-dog love, following him with their eyes and waiting for him to approach them to flirt up a storm. One of his newest crushes happened to be Miss Skylar Lynn, except this wasn't just an innocent schoolgirl crush for her—it went much deeper than that. It was her Twin Flame, and she knew the moment she laid eyes on him.

TWIN FLAMES DO EXIST

The purpose of a Twin Flame is to help us shed the ego, face our losses, and awaken our faith to the power of *The Silver Lights*. From the moment she laid eyes on Redmond, Skylar felt the earth beneath her legs move. It was the strongest magnetic earthquake that she had ever felt when she met a man, awakening her entire spirit to see her hidden fears and shadows even more. It was like she had known him for several lifetimes, and every time she looked at him, he became more like the mirror to her reflection of what she wanted to be.

Similarly, when he was in her presence, he started to feel a magnetic force pulling him closer to her. The moment he saw her from afar, it was as if something felt familiar, too close to home. It was not a lustful type of attraction, like he had the moment he met Ava Marie or the other porn features, but it was something that went beyond a physical and emotional connection. He felt, too, that they had a past soul connection in another lifetime. Even when he just glanced at her physical appearance: from her mannerisms in the way she spoke with her hands, to the way her honey-blonde hair touched her boob, to the way her almond-shaped eyes lit up when she spoke with humility just sent chills down his spine, so much that he had to walk to the bathroom to try to tell himself there was no such thing, even though deep down inside he was just feeding himself lies. In fact, he knew this woman more than anyone he was ever with in his current life, but he was not going to give into the power of his feelings in *The City of Dreams* until Skylar would begin to dance her way into a *Hollywood Dream*.

FADE OUT

FADE IN

Tony and Redmond are lost in conversation about Skylar's performance and first day at Silver Lights.

DIALOGUE

TONY: I'm actually quite surprised with how well she is taking to the pole and being topless.

REDMOND: Tee, are you kidding me?

TONY: Well, from the looks of her and her experience, it's not typical that we get someone like her through the doors of Silver Lights. She reminds me of a teacher or nurse. (*Laughs.*)

REDMOND: We have a few teachers and nurses here actually working part-time on the weekends. Amanda and Jacinda fall into both that category. I think you just really need to talk to her next time.

TONY: I spoke with her already.

REDMOND: She is a real star. She has a gift that I can see.

TONY: What are you talking about? You can see? Are you gifted with special powers like a real psychic that looks at a crystal ball and reads the future?

REDMOND: I can tell she is very different. I don't want to get into details.

TONY: She is different in that she looks like a secretary fantasy over a porn star!

REDMOND: I'm serious. Forget the secretary fantasy. She is going to make Silver Lights more than a strip club with her writing.

TONY: Are you on something?

REDMOND: Of course not. Just hear me out.

TONY: Fine, but what really makes you think this woman Skylar from the Midwest who has never stripped or worked in a gentlemen's club is going to make Silver Lights a household name?

REDMOND: In time you will see she is just different in a good way. She can give Silver Lights the national exposure it needs. I'm telling you her talent for writing could be what Silver Lights needs in terms of differentiating us from the typical strip clubs. Just think this could be Silver Lights chance to be on the big screen. An educated woman ready to give up her dreams by accident stumbles upon her starring role as an exotic dancer where dancing her way around drama gives her the breakthrough material she needs to write her Hollywood Dream.

TONY: Hollywood Dream? What nonsense are you speaking? I mean, she did mention she is a writer, but come on . . .

REDMOND: I did some investigating, and I found some of her published pieces on social media. And this girl is something else. She has a way with words. When I read some of her poems, I can feel her heart and soul in every piece so much that I can see it happening. I found out from a little spy that she is going to use her new role as Soleil to finish her first screenplay, *The City of Dreams*. It was on pause until now. I believe she has the talent to tell a great story and a fresh perspective in the world of nightlife and exotic entertainment. I can see the headline right now: "Premiere Gentlemen's Club Gives Woman a Chance to Dance Her Way into a Hollywood Dream."

TONY: So, what makes you think her screenplay will be picked up? Her chances of winning the lottery are better than that.

REDMOND: I can't tell you exactly how I know. I just have a strong intuition that she is the next big thing to come into the world of stripping, beyond the overdone asses and glorified Instagram models.

TONY: House Mom Shay did mention the other day she studied acting, too. When I had asked about her dance experience, Shay brought up a good point, that although Skylar was inexperienced, her acting skills would be an advantage over other dancers when it comes to dealing with difficult customers, and drama in the champagne rooms.

REDMOND: Exactly. You know my intuition is always right, and I have a strong feeling about Skylar. She is going to be the next big thing in Hollywood. Imagine if we actually helped contribute to her screenplay *Hollywood Dreams* by exposing her to more behind the scenes.

TONY: I see where you are going with this, but let's hold off for right now. I would like to wait at least a month before we introduce her to the underground world of Silver Lights.

REDMOND: Trust me, Tee. You know once I have a strong vision it's always spot-on. I was right when Frank Delucca of Gemstone Ventures & Hospitality bought out our former competitor, gangster Salvatore Marziano's share, and hired Steven Banks from City Group to run their whole enterprise.

TONY: Indeed you were, and now there is a big possibility Steven Banks may be merging or investing with Diamond Hospitality to make Silver Lights a national franchise.

REDMOND: From the moment I laid eyes on her, I have had a series of vivid dreams last night about her taking the world of stripping as we know it to mainstream and making it marketable to a PG audience.

TONY: Stripping being marketable for a PG audience? Are you out of your mind?

REDMOND: No, I'm not. I'm serious about this.

TONY: And your dreams should be about Barbie, not this woman.

REDMOND: Barbie will always be in my dreams and be my southern belle, but please listen to me because you are not hearing me out.

I have a very strong feeling she is going to make Silver Lights a worldwide name not just in the adult industry but in Hollywood, too.

TONY: Slow down, I'm hearing you about this woman's screenplay, *Hollywood Dreams*. This sounds great, but first things first, she must get comfortable with her cues, dialogue, and scenes as Soleil, and then we can revisit this in seven weeks. Capeesh?

REDMOND: Ok, that's fine.

TONY: Once I see she has taken to her new role and is selling champagne bottles with no problem, we can explore giving her character more direction and information from behind the scenes.

REDMOND: Trust me, it's going to be the best future decision that you will make.

TONY: If I can find a way to get John Marino's sister Victoria out of my bachelor pad, that will be the best decision I make.

REDMOND: Things aren't good?

TONY: You can say that. I prefer not to discuss it, just like you prefer not to address the rumors about Amber Ray.

Redmond looks down at his phone.

TONY: Who is it?

REDMOND: It's Barbie. We need to talk Sunday about the "dirty martini special."

TONY: Usual spot, and come in a half hour before the club opens.

REDMOND: Ok, I have to run. I'm getting another message from Michael. They need me in the back champagne room.

Tony turns his attention back to Skylar's performance. Her dance had come to an end. She quickly made her way offstage, heading towards the dressing room. She sat down again in front of the mirror, taking one last stare at herself. She began to sigh with relief that her first ever performance was behind her. She was no longer a "virgin" to exotic dancing, and her days of ballet slippers and tap shoes were traded in for a swanky pair of Silver Heels. She couldn't believe she really did it! She actually made it through her first real performance dancing topless in a gentlemen's club. In that moment, she truly felt like a star. Nothing anyone could say or do could steal that glamorous moment. Not even the eviction warning that she had received the day of her audition, warning her she had only seven days to pay February's rent in full, otherwise she would have a week to find a new address.

She couldn't really put into words the feelings she experienced after the performance, but it was warm, tingly, and peaceful. It was the warmest and most relaxed feeling she had experienced yet from the guidance of The Silver Lights. It was this paranormal experience that The Silver Lights kept on portraying in her scenes that allowed her "dirty dancing" with the pole to be her newest instrument in playing out her lyrics to continuing her Hollywood Dreams.

This time, as Skylar focused on her expression in the mirror, her shadow was no longer in sight. There was only light in her scenes and warmth surrounding her character. You can see her new character

Soleil had transformed Skylar's spirit into a heavenly goddess that radiated strength, embodied love, and reflected faith. But would this new spirit of a heavenly goddess be enough for Soleil to master her different scenes of "dirty dancing"?

FADE OUT

CHAPTER 9
DIRTY DANCING

Skylar's first taste of "dirty dancing" was in 1987 from her favorite movie, *Dirty Dancing*, where acclaimed actors Jennifer Grey and Patrick Swayze took the spotlight with their hot romance and dance choreography by winning over a quiet resort in the Catskills. From that day on, every time she watched *Dirty Dancing*, she knew she was destined to be a star. Not just any Hollywood star, but a shining star of inspiration.

Every time Skylar saw *Dirty Dancing*, a stronger force took hold of her spirit. The force awoke her character pumping faster through her veins, and igniting a fire of passion in her doe-shaped eyes. It was evident that every time she jumped, skipped, and hopped back to her *Playground of Dreams*, the recurring flashback of those final scenes from *Dirty Dancing* would enter her vision, leaving her in the most surreal state. The feelings that she experienced every time she imagined herself in the role of Jennifer Grey's character left her closer to her vision of becoming a star. The feelings of serenity and joy that came into her heart and soul as she recaptured those final scenes began to allow herself to surrender her whole being to the source coming from *The Silver Lights.*

It was this magnetic force from *The Silver Lights* that planted seeds of faith in Skylar's new character, Soleil, the exotic dancer. No matter how many times Skylar heard and felt the loud percussion of her character defects, the magnetic force from *The Silver Lights* would always shine over her defects, bringing harmony to the beauty of her own voice.

Little did Skylar know that the beauty of her voice was awaiting her in the dialogue of the final act. She was finally ready to play her new character "Soleil" with ease, conviction, and a bit of sexiness as she was on her way towards building a sizzling reel.

THE SIZZLING REEL

Skylar was still gathering herself after her performance by touching up her makeup, brushing her hair, and applying her coconut body spray. She felt relieved that she lived up to her new role. Now that the first part of her night was done, she had to face the hardest part yet, facing her fears of "dirty dancing." To reassure her new character Soleil that she could continue the night with a smash, she kept reminding herself of the paranormal experience and visions she had when watching the finale of *Dirty Dancing.* If Skylar could keep this mystical and powerful vision intact throughout the night, she would be well on her way towards building a sizzling reel in her next feature, *Hollywood Dreams.*

So many questions kept running aimlessly through Skylar's head. Would she be able to dance up to par performing the role of an exotic dancer, while also incorporating stripper traits into her new scenes? Some of these traits were sex appeal, being flirty, having good dance rhythm, and being a chameleon with different situations. Would she be able to take her sex appeal and great dance rhythm a bit further with the customer by trying to upsell a lap dance into a champagne room? And would she be able to transfer her paranormal experience from those flashback scenes in *Dirty Dancing* to enjoying parts of her new dialogue that were foreign to her, such as lap dancing and champagne rooms with strangers? How would she be able to make a real connection within a short time to get them to spend money and time with her in a champagne room? All these questions were racing through her head at the speed of light, and meanwhile her first introduction with Michael Donahue and Lola was seconds away, and her third meeting with her Twin Flame Redmond, who made her heart skip a beat.

From the moment she laid eyes on Redmond's rugged country boy looks and heard his first words, "Miss Skylar you look lovely," in his southern accent, it just melted her heart. She knew right there and then there was something special between her and Redmond. She immediately read up on Twin Flames, and everything from the description concluded Redmond was indeed hers. The indescribable feeling you have with no words exchanged, just thoughts and deep eye contact. The feeling that half of your soul is within someone else was the experience she felt during her first encounter with Redmond. Never had she experienced this feeling with any of her past boyfriends or crushes. An unspoken connection, an exchange of words from the soul, and deep eye contact is all she needed to know that Redmond was her soul connection from another lifetime. The way he looked at her with his ocean-blue eyes and the way he greeted her with his masculine hands wasn't the first time she felt his touch. Her soul just knew his spirit from somewhere else. The vibration from him was there, too. The way he choked up halfway in their conversation from nerves. The uneasiness that he felt when he was in her presence because he, too, had never experienced any feeling like this. She could also see the turmoil of the club drama building up in his eyes. She knew that within weeks Redmond would be given the opportunity to possibly turn his back on Tony, and Silver Lights for a posh life on Wall Street.

Still although she read him like a book, Skylar felt nervous butterflies in her stomach every time he passed, wondering if he was attracted to her on a physical level. In a pool of hundreds of beautiful woman who resembled pin-ups and glorified Instagram models, Skylar definitely stood out. Her body was natural: real boobs, lean, muscular legs, and a small bubble butt. Her body did resemble a professional dancer or yoga teacher. Her face looked slightly exotic with thick eyebrows, full lips, high cheekbones, and a narrow face. She definitely didn't look like a pin-up model, but she was exotically attractive.

"Skylar," House Mom Shay called, "Redmond and Michael Martinez are ready for your last part of the night."

"Great, I will be right there," Skylar responded.

Skylar looked once more into her reflection, and this time she closed her eyes and took a deep breath to visualize the final scenes from *Dirty Dancing*, so her chakras and third eye would be aligned and open to whatever experience awaited her in the final act. She turned her back to the mirror and grabbed her clutch, heading into her final act in *The City of Dreams*.

IT'S ALL ABOUT THE CHAMPAGNE

Time was ticking down to her last scenes of the night that would make or break her starring role.

Redmond, Michael Donahue, and Lola were all in the restaurant bar area waiting for her arrival.

Michael Donahue had quite the reputation as the ladies' man at Silver Lights, a former Playboy and professional athlete. His thick Boston accent and charming demeanor sold many champagne rooms. Michael Donahue had stumbled upon Silver Lights by luck. After the merger with Diamond Hospitality, Tony had more funds to allocate towards restructuring the human resources of the club. Being a traditional Italian, Tony immediately turned to his family to fill some of the new jobs at the club. Tony reached out right away to his close friend and distant cousin Michael. He enticed Michael by saying that his job as the head champagne host would be a lucrative opportunity with a large potential in the near future if Silver Lights got the funding from Frank Delucca's firm, Gemstone Hospitality.

To seal the deal as a head champagne host, he offered Michael a quarterly percentage of all the liquor sales sold at Silver Lights. Michael Donahue, a former Wall Street bad boy with deep Irish and Italian roots in the mafia, resembled a middle-aged Leo DiCaprio. His former days before Silver Lights was a story of contradictions. One story read "Young Rookie Pitcher Signs with Boston Minors," whereas another story read "Magic Mike Performs . . ." When the baseball headline didn't work out, Michael got trapped in the seedy world of Magic Mike and a life of insider trading. Rumor has it that his days on the Vegas strip mimicked the movie *Casino*, and he left his bad boy image behind for church and his new wife, Grace. Luckily, Michael escaped a life of prison for insider trading because of his mafia roots and political ties.

He was left with no choice but to fly away from Vegas, leaving his days of partying, trading, and his playboy life behind, moving back to the East Coast. He claimed his bad boy ways were far behind him, and through his newfound faith in Christianity and his mandatory twelve-step program, he became reformed. It was in twelve-step program that he met his beautiful Spanish wife, Grace, a former *Sports Illustrated* model who graced the editorial pages of *Vogue*, and who also got tangled in world of sex, drugs, and rock n' roll. The world of super modeling introduced her to blow, keeping her skinny and giving her the right covers.

When Michael was not in the club, his wingman, Frankie Martinez, part Italian and Spanish with looks that resembled Marc Consuelos, was second in charge of all champagne rooms. They called him "Smooth Frankie" around the club because he was smooth in selling champagne rooms and schmoozing with top customers every night, selling around 15,000 dollars a week in liquor sales to contribute to over one-fourth of all bottle sales last quarter. He dreamt of getting a music contract one day so he could travel the world performing. He saw Silver Lights as the perfect place for him to break into the business. His job at Silver Lights gave him exposure to heavy hitters weekly and *Page Six* celebrities who would frequent the champagne rooms.

Then there was Lola, or at least that's what she goes by at Silver Lights. A Korean-American in her late twenties with looks that resembled Lucy Liu, except she had two mountains of fake boobs popping out. Rumors were circulating around the club that she overplays her Asian card by focusing on extreme fetish to upsell champagne rooms. She is the premiere seller at Silver Lights and stumbled upon exotic dancing after a one-time film assignment, and a bad breakup turned into an ongoing four-year party of fetish stories. Initially, she found herself looking for ways to discover a kinkier version of herself in the club through her exploration of writing and film after being dumped by her ex-boyfriend for a younger and kinkier version of her. Of all places, Lola, really known by her family as Lucy, came from a strict Tiger mom and Asian upbringing had found her real voice by being "Lola," the exotic dancer. She dreamed that one day to be a director of blockbuster movies. Her days of working at Silver Lights blurred her dreams slightly as she got caught up in the unfolding drama of sex, drugs, and rock n' roll cooking up in the champagne rooms.

So you can see the two misfits, Skylar and Lola, had a bond right from the start. Two educated woman from working class families who found their next starring roles as exotic dancers in an unassuming club called Silver Lights.

ACT VI, SCENE 1
CHAMPAGNE FUN

INT: BAR AREA

FADE IN

Skylar heads to Redmond, and he pulls out the chair. Lola and Michael Donahue are sitting down.

DIALOGUE

REDMOND: Darling, congrats! You are now family. (*Leans over to hug Skylar.*)

SKYLAR: (*Takes a seat.*) It still seems like a daydream.

REDMOND: The daydream isn't over, so don't forget that.

SKYLAR: Yes, Redmond. (*flirty*)

REDMOND: Soleil, please call me Red. (*Laughs.*)

SKYLAR: Ok, Red. Who is this beautiful woman? (*looking at Lola*)

REDMOND: This is Lola, our premiere seller at *Silver Lights*.

LOLA: Pleasure to meet you. I think once you get familiar with how things are run here and get comfortable selling champagne rooms, you're going to create some fireworks!

SKYLAR: Hopefully it's in the champagne room. That's where all the fun and green paper happen, I hear.

LOLA: Green paper and fun is happening everywhere. You just need the right skill set. Stick with me, and you will have no problem.

SKYLAR: Skill set as in a great booty shake?

REDMOND: That's where I was about to go. Yes, you need to perfect the booty shake. All kidding aside, Soleil, I paired you with Lola because she is the best, and I think you two are going to work well together.

LOLA: I'm looking forward to working with you. I think we have a bit in common. I overheard from Shay that you're aspiring Hollywood screenwriter and actress. I actually went to film school at NYU and received a degree in film and psychology. Now I'm putting my degree to full force. (*Chuckles.*)

REDMOND: You are, because every day here there is an exciting story taking place with interesting characters, different scenes, and one feature story.

LOLA: True that. There is always one feature story cooking up. I love your comparison!

REDMOND: That's why I'm here to provide you guys with support, motivation, and security.

LOLA: I don't know what I would do without you. Soleil, this is the best place to work anywhere in the city or the state of New York if you are going to be an exotic dancer. Red really goes out of his way to make us feel safe, relaxed, and well compensated. Just listen to the managers and follow my cues; we are here to help you succeed in your new role. First things first, your role is going to be my distant cousin from my mom's side, and you are less than one-quarter Asian.

SKYLAR: So I am a quarter Asian?

LOLA: Less than a quarter, since your eyes are a bit bigger. Haha. You're going to play up that story if customers get curious and ask more questions about why we are working together. It's not typical that I work one-on-one with someone all week, especially when I get my regulars that come in requesting me. Let me tell you one last thing, since you studied acting and are an aspiring actress?

SKYLAR: Yes, I am.

LOLA. This will be your starring role. Every day with new scenes, new characters, and new plots, you're going to have to play the role of "Soleil" with ease. You're going to be more real than you ever imagined, but also out of character at any time where the drama is boiling up in the champagne rooms.

SKYLAR: I have a question that may be off topic. Is there any fantasy involved in selling a champagne room?

LOLA: That's a great question. The fantasy experience is what draws the customer to come in, and when they step into a champagne room, well, the fantasy comes to life. It's not as X-rated as it sounds, cousin. It's actually more like a cross between PG-13 and rated R.

SKYLAR: I love your sense of humor. (*Giggles.*)

LOLA: Sense of humor is super important as a dancer because it will bait in the biggest spender over looks, surprisingly. It's all about connecting to the customer. Yes, sex appeal sells, but everyone here has the sex appeal. It's the humor, connection, and fantasy you create that will get you the most bucks at the end of the night. First things first, you are now my cousin, Soleil, and you're going to watch my cues, follow my lead, and understudy me, and then create a storyline for the scenes tonight. Do you think you can do that?

SKYLAR: I can!

LOLA: One last thing is that you must get to know the business here as well as the customer that walks through this door. Understanding operations and your customer's desires will be the difference between a hundred dollars a night to over a thousand dollars a night.

SKYLAR: (Nods in agreement.) It can't be much harder than trying to sell actual real estate. I can at least get naked to seduce the customer in buying a champagne room. (*Laughs.*)

MICHAEL: Soleil, don't get caught up in the stripper stereotypes because that mentality will only make you get stuck. You need to have an open mind, erasing any stereotypes you have learned up to now. The less labels and judgments you have about your own role as a stripper, the greater possibility you have in excelling here, and the bigger your bank account will be. Trust me, Soleil.

SKYLAR: I do, but part of me finds it difficult to trust easily.

MICHAEL: I understand, but we get many girls like yourself through the doors every day, and the ones that don't trust in Silver Lights— you don't want to know what happens to them.

SKYLAR: What happens?

MICHAEL: They go back to their struggles and, for some, they end up in worse situations than when they started. Whether or not you believe this is true, trust me, Soleil, you will witness it with your own eyes the longer you work here. You will see dancers from all walks of life come and go through this door, some faster than others, but some will dance their way to the top.

(Lola and Redmond all look in agreement.)

LOLA: Soleil, listen to Michael. He is the top seller for the club the past two years, producing over a few million in liquor sales, which is unheard of. (Lola looks at Michael in a flirty way.)

MICHAEL DONAHUE: The customers that walk through this door or the big groups that come in and kick it on the weekend are looking for entertainment beyond the tits and ass scenarios you see on TV. The thing that separates Silver Lights from the standard run-of-the-mill clubs is the high level of hospitality and entertainment we provide to each and every customer that walk through the door.

REDMOND: Although we drive our business from liquor sales and hospitality, the exotic entertainers are the icing on the cake—without the sweet flavor that the exotic entertainers provide, our club would taste bland!

LOLA: Yes, and the sweeter we make the flavor, the bigger appetite the customer has when returning, and that means they will make it rain!

SKYLAR: I love the analogy of equating dessert to the different flavors of the dancers.

MICHAEL: Love it!

SKYLAR: A refreshing flavor of sweetness, so what flavor, cuz, are you going to be?

LOLA: I love how you're talking already. I'm going to be bold in flavor, full of rich drama that will really spice up the night.

MICHAEL: Ladies, you are making me hungry!

Redmond is getting a call on the phone. Everyone becomes quiet. The call is from Steven Banks.

You can't miss Steven Banks the moment he walks in the club. He is a middle-aged, stocky American with a beer belly, and his outlandish remarks and eccentric sense of humor make him quite the character of the drama for the night. Whenever he comes, the storylines become more exciting, humorous, and of course, full of fetish dialogue.

PHONE CALL

REDMOND: Steven, so nice to hear from you. So, you are coming by tomorrow night with some possible investors?

STEVEN BANKS: (*from the phone*) Yes, I am. Can you reserve the Howard Stern champagne room around 10:00 PM? I want the full monte! Also, I'm a bit hungry for some Asian appetizers. If you can bring that kinky Asian, I think her name was Lola . . .

REDMOND: Yes, it's Lola.

Lola looks at Redmond with curiosity and excitement as he says her name.

REDMOND: (*Phone call continues.*) Sounds good! I will make it happen. See you tomorrow night.

PHONE CALL ENDS

REDMOND: You guys, I have to cut this meeting to an end now. If you have any questions, Soleil, just direct them to Lola or Michael.

Redmond leaves the room in a hurry. Michael looks at his phone, and he is receiving texts from his former Wall Street trader, colleague, and friend, Brooks Kennedy. Brooks comes directly from Kennedy family lineage, being a distant cousin. His ancestor's roots are deeply mixed into the politics of New York City. His clean-cut, all-American looks, sandy brown hair, and ocean blue eyes resemble famous hunk Jamie Dornan. He tends to frequent Silver Lights discreetly by coming in through the back door, and reserving the Howard Stern champagne room from time to time. It is the most private room for top spenders and celebrities at Silver Lights. His company, Onyx Equities is the second biggest hedge fund firm in New York, besides billionaire Charles Marziano's firm, Sapphire Investments. Sapphire has been number one for the past decade on the exchange. The only thing that could take Sapphire Investments' number one slot would be one of the two options: exposure to insider trading or corporate espionage, and the second would be if he had direct relations or dealings with New York's biggest crime family, the Marziano family. Of all names, the richest guy in all of New York City with one of the biggest hedge funds coincidentally has the same name as the notorious crime family.

Charles Marziano has always been vigilant in maintaining an honest and worthy reputation as a businessman, defending his last name as having no direct ties to the Marziano crime family.

The text Michael receives:

Hey Michael, I need to reserve The Howard Stern Champagne Room tomorrow at midnight. I have a big deal cooking for Onyx Equities.

Michael is quietly panicking because Steven Banks is booked tomorrow night for the champagne room, creating a huge dilemma for the management of Silver Lights. The question becomes who is more important in terms of receiving VIP treatment for Silver Lights tomorrow: is it their biggest cash cow, Brooks Kennedy, or the assumption that they are going to be landing an investment from Gemstone Hospitality that could change the future brand of Silver Lights? The risk of losing Brooks Kennedy's business could be detrimental to the overall earnings of Silver Lights, resulting in a quarterly deficit of 200,000 dollars.

You can see how agitated Michael was becoming.

LOLA: What's wrong, Michael?

MICHAEL: Nothing really, except the fact that Brooks Kennedy is coming in tomorrow and wants the Howard Stern champagne room at midnight, around the same time Steven Banks will be in it.

LOLA: That's two hours until he gets there, and it should be enough time for Steven Banks to leave.

MICHAEL: Lola, are you serious? You know how carried away Steven Banks gets in the room with his foot fetish.

SKYLAR: Foot fetish? Geez Louise.

LOLA: Skylar, it's not as bad as you think. (*Giggles.*) Michael, I will make sure he is ready way before then. I will speed up the wet feet party. I have a few tricks up my sleeve to speed up his foot fantasy so he's not in the room all night, although it would be quite comical to entertain them both.

MICHAEL: Come on, Lola.

SKYLAR: I'm worried about tomorrow.

LOLA: Ignore this problem. I promise you everything will be fine.

Skylar nods her head.

MICHAEL: I need to get going to make sure we have a plan B if for some reason the Steve Banks room exceeds the hour and a half time limit tomorrow.

LOLA: It won't. Are you going to let Red know?

MICHAEL: Of course, and I'm going to see if we can call NYC's hottest porn star Amber Ray to come in tomorrow for plan B.

Did Skylar just hear that a "porn star" would be making a special appearance tomorrow? Her jaw dropped. She never thought in a million years she would be working side-by-side with a famous porn star. Not only would she have to step up her game in the world of Exotic Entertainment, but she would really have to get into character, so speaking her lines in her new scenes with a real porn star would come naturally.

SKYLAR LYNN: (*Fearfully*) Porn star?

MICHAEL: (*Sarcastically*) Relax, Soleil, we are not having the actual porn going on. We have feature adult performers that come in weekly and do dance performances like you on stage and mingle with our top customers in the champagne rooms.

SKYLAR LYNN: So, there is no porn-type activity in the champagne rooms?

MICHAEL: Of course not. Come on, that would be illegal, and we can shut the club down.

LOLA: Soleil, just relax and have fun. You have nothing to worry about. Try to follow my lead. Another suggestion: guys like it when you act sweet as cherry pie!

SKYLAR: Sweet as cherry pie, hmmmm.

Skylar looks at Lola and nods with a lack of confidence. All three leave the bar area with Michael heading to the office and Skylar following Lola's lead like a little puppy toward the front area of the stage, where customers are sitting.

Part of Skylar's character is frozen with fear, while another part of herself is burning with excitement. Would tomorrow's scenes at Silver Lights be the storyline to writing her Hollywood Dream, or would the room have the typical drama of sex, drugs, and rock n' roll? Would the escalated storyline cooking up between Steven Banks's time in the Howard Stern champagne room interfere with Silver Lights' biggest spender, Brooks Kennedy? And more importantly, would she leave her slippers behind for a life of Silver Heels and real dialogue to fuel her Hollywood Dreams? So many thoughts were running rampantly through her head as her name echoed across the dance room. The voice from afar came from a young woman who looked exactly like Anastasia, Skylar's real estate colleague.

In panic mode, Skylar immediately excused herself to Lola, saying she needed to use the restroom, and just like that as Skylar went towards the restroom, the sound of rock n' roll came across the speakers playing the song "Cherry Pie."

CHAPTER 10
SWEET AS CHERRY PIE

As Skylar took refuge in the bathroom stall, fear began to tremble in her hands, and her whole body began to shake like an earthquake. Once again, she was taken back to her own internal storm of trepidation. She continued to panic at the thought that someone behind the scenes from her role as an extra on the cold streets of NYC would recognize her.

She kept reminding herself that her new role as Soleil, the exotic dancer would be part of her storyline to writing her *Hollywood Dreams*. With the power of her *Hollywood Dreams* right in front of her, and the powerful vision from her days of watching *Dirty Dancing*, Skylar began to concentrate on her meditation, shifting her focus back to *The Playground of Dreams* as *The Silver Lights* began to prevail once again, conquering her darkest shadows of fear. With each inhale, her exhales got lighter and longer. Each breath became more liberating than the next as she began to forget the dialogue of panic. The deeper she got into her visions, the closer she was able see herself as a star, and the calmer her whole spirit became. You can see the peace had settled on her face, and glimmered upon her smile. She began to feel both enlightened and uplifted at the same time as she began to channel the energy from *The Silver Lights* towards igniting the dance magic of the *Silver Heels*. She took one last breath and felt a tingling sensation in her feet as the silent rhythm of her soul began to connect with the internal rhythm of the *Silver Heels*, guiding her to walk outside the stall.

This time as she stared in the mirror, she saw not just a star, but a fascinating character that would be her breakthrough role towards dancing her way in the direction of her *Hollywood Dream*.

THE CHAMPAGNE ADVENTURE CONTINUES

Skylar left the bathroom and was determined more than ever to make her new role, Soleil, a star, no matter what drama was cooking up in the champagne rooms. Those comforting words, "sweet as cherry pie," kept echoing in the back of her head as she was ready to squash any fears still plaguing her, especially since she was in the bathroom for 20 minutes after thinking she saw Anastasia. As she got back to the front area, the image of Anastasia was nowhere in sight.

Phew, Skylar thought. One less fire she had to put out.

"Soleil, come over here," echoed from the upper VIP seating area. The voice was coming from Lola. She was with another dancer who went by the name of Brianna. The two had worked together on occasion. She had the most exotic looks at Silver Lights, a physical resemblance between Rhianna and Alicia Keys. No wonder she went with the name Brianna.

She had been born in the Caribbean to a black mother and a white father, who left before she was born. Rumors circulated that part of her DNA was linked directly to a famous political family and that her mom, who was a beauty queen at the time, had an affair in the Virgin Islands with someone from a well-known political circle. Her mom had been a beauty queen and attracted the top celebrities and politicians that went to St. Martin. From a young age, she was groomed to be around these men who flew into the island for vacation and high-profile events. This taste of American luxury left her thirsty for the American Dream. After Brianna was born, her mother got an opportunity to live in New York City and further her education in policy and administration working for the government, eventually leading her to a confidential position working with NYC Mayor Thomas Mahoney.

One night, after Brianna and her mom had gotten in a heated argument about her choosing a singing career over school, Brianna found herself searching for a path to continue to feed her dreams. The money that she was spending to produce and market her own music was dwindling her mother's savings and her future college tuition. So Brianna, like Skylar and Lola, found herself auditioning for her next starring role center stage at Silver Lights.

Shortly after joining Silver Lights, she found herself walking a tightrope between the world of Jane Citizen and the world of Exotic Entertainment, camera-ready for the escapades of sex, drugs, and rock n' roll. Ironically, Brianna, who grew up with a strong Christian faith, felt the most at home at Silver Lights, where she could be herself on stage performing like a star to her favorites and feeling closer to her dreams of becoming a recording artist.

Silver Lights was the first place that allowed her to tap more into her performing side. Her real dream was to become a famous R&B singer, signed by a top record label as she danced her way to the top. Like Skylar and Lola, her family and friends had no clue about her second life.

Skylar walked over to the three business guys who looked like they worked on Wall Street. They were all dressed in pressed and tailored suits. One of them stood out as the ringleader. His name was John Marino, but they called him "Buck" because he had a way of bringing in the bucks on Wall Street. Born in the Bronx to a working class family, he worked his way all the way up to the top. A self-made Wall Street tycoon in his early forties with looks of Al Pacino, he had what seemed like the picture-perfect life. A model wife, a beautiful son, and a penthouse overlooking Park Street on the Upper East Side, however all wasn't perfect in John's life because he had a sex addiction. Instead of using escort agencies or having random affairs from Tinder, he went straight to Silver Lights, where he could be himself and let his sexual desires run free. He was a regular at Silver Lights frequently coming in after client dinner meetings. To him, Silver Lights was a place for him to relax after the hustle and bustle on the exchange, and keep his sexual appetite satisfied.

His high stress job kept him on his feet as he was always waiting for the next big deal or stock to land in his lap. He was quick to respond to business texts, emails, and anything that was urgent. He was second in charge of the largest hedge fund in NYC, Sapphire Investments. The rumor was his founder, Charles Marziano, known as "The Beast on Wall Street" was running for mayor in 2020, against Thomas Mahoney. The other two guys who came in with

John Marino were his posse, Philip Delfonte and Craig Peters, who worked directly under John in the same firm.

All of a sudden, Skylar entered the scene trying to act somewhat intoxicated, like she is the life of the "party," as the attention is directed towards her.

ACT VI, SCENE 2
WALL STREET PARTY BOYS

INT: VIP SECTION

FADE IN

DIALOGUE

LOLA: Soleil, just the person I have in mind. I want to introduce you to the legend John Marino. Better known as the "Beast of Wall Street."

JOHN: No, Charlie Marziano is the "Beast of Wall Street." I'm just one of his cronies. I'm John, pleasure to meet you, Soleil.

SKYLAR: Billionaires come here?

BRIANNA: Girl, you have no idea. Billionaires, celebs, and *New York Post* page six stories are made here.

SKYLAR: Wow, that's so dope!

BRIANNA: Girl, don't be getting star struck on me!

SKYLAR: Who says I'm getting star struck? I just want to have fun!

BRIANNA: Ok good, because remember, you are not their groupie, but someone they can escape into a fantasy with.

SKYLAR: I love fantasies. I'm big into role-playing.

JOHN: Baby, you are talking my language.

BRIANNA: Fantasies are going to bring you lots of green paper.

LOLA: Bri, stop it. You are feeding her too much information. She just needs to come out of her shell.

SKYLAR: I am out of my shell. Come on . . . (*Dances sexy in front of the three guys.*) I love how I am here to be a sex-ay fantasy! (*Looks at Craig Peter.*)

CRAIG: The sexy fantasy is in the champagne room. (*Looks at John.*)

Overwhelmed with her newfound sensuality from exploring her character Soleil, she feels compelled to move closer to the men.

SKYLAR: So, gentlemen, when are we going to get really naughty in the champagne room?

PHILIP: Well, John, being the notorious playboy that he is will be your first customer.

CRAIG: That's true.

Lola and Brianna smile.

LOLA: Craig, stop causing drama . . .

JOHN: Craig, don't put any bad ideas in this angel's head.

Skylar gets to the core of her character by bringing out her most seductive side yet. Lola and Brianna are a bit shocked at how well she is playing her new role. She goes to John and takes a seat on his lap. She begins to touch him playfully, in a way that is suggestive for performing her first lap dance of the night.

SKYLAR: Hey, Johnny Boy. I'm ready to live it up with you in the champagne room. Will you be my first? Pretty please?

JOHN: Baby girl, I'm going to take a rain check tonight because I have an early business meeting. Let's do a few lap dances this time, and next time I roll in, I promise I will be your first.

LOLA: John you are not going to be her first. Steven Banks is . . .

JOHN: Steven Banks is not what I call a "first." His experience is "wet feet" from what I hear.

SKYLAR: Wet feet? So how are they getting wet?

LOLA: (*turns to Skylar, and then John*) Really, Let's forget that I just heard you say that and John, leave Steven Banks alone. He is a harmless guy that is starved for some special attention.

PHILIP: Special attention. The guy has extreme fetish fantasies with feet. But on a serious note, he is not harmless. You haven't heard the rumors.

LOLA: What rumors?

PHILIP: He is a key player associated with the Louis Mazarati Ponzi scheme.

CRAIG: I can back that up. I ran into someone that works with Louis, and he is being charged with all counts of fraud and embezzlement. I'm not sure if I can vouch one hundred percent that Steven Banks is part of the whole scheme, though.

Skylar is at a loss for words from what she is hearing. A Page Six story was seriously in the works between Steven Banks being a possible con man working under the biggest hospitality and venture firms in the United States. If that were true, he would be using dirty money for the expansion of the Silver Lights brand, leaving Silver Lights with more drama than it could imagine. On the flip side, this could be only rumors about Steven Banks being part of the Mazarati Ponzi scheme. The juicy drama brewing up was fueling the storyline for her second feature, Hollywood Dreams.

Skylar's face flushed and her heart began to race faster from all the juicy information she was getting to play with in her new storyline. Although she was starting to dance her way in the direction of her Hollywood Dream, she would first have to master her new voice amongst the dialogue of drama.

If she was really good at her new role, she would capture the headlines, but not be caught in the middle of the boiling drama of white-collar crimes, deceit, and love affairs.

Lola noticed Skylar's anxious state and went in to intervene, flirting with Skylar in a way that would get all three men excited.

LOLA: John. It's your lucky night because you are going to get a double dose of fantasy . . .

JOHN: Wow, a double dose of fantasy. What did I do to deserve this?

LOLA: Just being you, baby.

CRAIG: What about me? I'm getting super hungry for a sweet fantasy?

BRIANNA: What about me, Craig? (*She flaunts her boobs in his face.*) I'm not exactly yesterday's dessert.

CRAIG: Of course not. I will take a few dances.

John, Lola, and Skylar, as well as Brianna and Craig, all head to the couch area, while Philip stays in the lounge area to smoke a cigar. Lola begins to dance on the right side of John, while Skylar is on the left side of him. Both prepare to get in a straddle-type position, slowly moving their hips to the music as Lola faces Skylar. Both are dancing seductively on John's lap with one foot on the ground and the other on the lap dance couch, maintaining or at least trying to keep a three-inch distance from John's groin. The Silver Lights rule was that all table dances on the floor must have three-inch distance between the dancer and customer; however, when top spenders came into the club, this rule tended to be overlooked.

As the music gets louder and the beats get faster, the two girls begin to get in sync while playfully touching and teasing John. Lola begins to whisper something dirty in John's ear.

JOHN: Oh yeah, baby.

Skylar immediately becomes a puppet to Lola's lap dance, following her cues, and shifting positions based on her body language. Lola begins to straddle-dance John from the front, while Skylar follows Lola's cue from behind, creating a dancing sandwich. Skylar is listening to the beats and, in the back of her head, tries to maintain a "sweet as cherry pie" image while following Lola's cues.

John was beginning to feel the effects of his whiskey shots and Roman Cokes. His face is getting flushed red, and he is starting to get a bit aroused from the double dancing.

LOLA: (*Turning around and whispering to Skylar*) Switch positions and now straddle him.

Lola slowly moves out of the straddle position while maintaining her rhythm to the music and still keeping John's interest. She was teasing him in such a way that John didn't even notice the swapping of positions as Lola went to the back, and Skylar moved to the front.

In astonishment, but still maintaining her composure, Skylar still couldn't believe her own eyes that she was dancing her first lap dance, and it wasn't scary. The beats of the music and Lola's guidance made it feel natural. She can tell John is getting extremely turned on by the sultry dance moves, as he started rubbing her neck and shoulders, and then moved his hands in a nonchalant way towards her breast. Her first reaction was to pull away, but she just went with it and grabbed his hand in an affectionate way, moving it towards her hips.

JOHN: (Whispers) Hey, baby, I want to get you as excited as I'm getting.

SKYLAR: Baby, I'm getting really excited.

She continues to move her hips in the straddle position back and forth. She couldn't believe the words that were coming out of her mouth, calling him "Baby" and telling him she was getting excited. John continues to touch her more, and then Lola comes back to the front, grabbing Skylar's hand and leading her about two footsteps in front of John as the two begin to dance erotically with each other in order to tempt John to spend more. They face the front of the stage, with their booties facing John, doing their booty shake the best they can. Suddenly the song ended, and the girls turned around facing John. As he is about to reach his wallet, the DJ announces that champagne rooms are half off.

John stops and then looks at Lola.

JOHN: How much do I owe you?

LOLA: Well, you owe us forty dollars apiece for the two-song set.

JOHN: *(gets out his wallet)* Girls, here is a tip for the outstanding dance.

LOLA: John, did you just hear that they announced half off champagne rooms?

JOHN: I can't tonight, Lola. I have a big meeting in the morning.

BRIANNA: Meetings can always be rescheduled.

JOHN: Not this type of meeting. Now it's past my curfew.

LOLA: Wait, When are we going to see you again, baby? *(She puts her arms around him.)*

JOHN: If this deal comes through, it will be soon, girls.

John hears a beeping coming from his phone and takes a few steps back from Lola to see the text. It's a high-alert text. The only high-alert texts that John receives are from the man himself, Charles Marziano. It reads,

You better have everything perfect tomorrow for the Precision Instruments meeting. I just got word from the Vice President of Finance, Camden Roberts that their stocks are doubling in the next month. This could mean a huge bonus for you and your team. I'm talking not just millions, but hundreds of millions.

Suddenly, John's face lights up as if he won the lottery.

LOLA: It looks like someone received good news.

JOHN: It's nothing, just work related, but I do need to get out of here. But I'm serious—there may be a celebration party the next time I walk through.

BRIANNA: I love celebration parties.

SKYLAR: The best part is the cake!

LOLA: I hope it's as sweet as cherry pie.

Over the speakers, Warrant's "Cherry Pie" starts playing again.

SKYLAR: Wow, déjà vu. Lola, you must have a superpower we don't know about.

LOLA: Don't you know, Soleil, the song "Cherry Pie" is the stripper anthem here?

The girls start giggling while John heads away from them in the direction towards where Philip is sitting. Philip looks a bit stressed and tense.

JOHN: What's wrong?

PHILIP: John, I just found out my wife Cassandra is having an affair with someone from Brooks Kennedy's firm, of all people.

JOHN: How do you know?

PHILIP: Look at my phone, there are pictures of her making out with someone from his firm. Bradley Ross, from the Smith firm is going use a facial recognition database to find out who this is.

JOHN: I'm really sorry about this, but you need to get this straightened out ASAP. Why didn't you say something to me?

PHILIP: You know me, I don't like to broadcast my life. I knew something wasn't right, so I hired this private investigator to follow her. She was coming home super late, saying her work meetings were running behind due to international calls. I looked one night at her phone and noticed a weird text from a contact labeled "Boss." There wasn't much dialogue between them. They were just one-word sentences like "Completed" or "meeting in the Am." I asked her who "Boss" was, and she said it had to with the new projects she was consulting with from China.

JOHN: It could possibly interfere with our largest investment.

PHILIP: What are you talking about?

JOHN: Precision Instruments. You have heard of them?

Philip: They are Onyx Equities' biggest fund.

JOHN: Yes, and I just got a message from Charles Marziano that Precision Instruments is having second thoughts about their fund with Onyx Equities, and want a second opinion on their valuation.

PHILIP: I'm not surprised. I have been telling you for months their stocks are volatile since joining Onyx.

JOHN: Shh, lower your voice. Do not repeat this to anyone. The kicker is, he has an insider person from the company named Camden Roberts giving him confidential information that their stock is going to double with the launch of their new software platform *Galaxy.*

Meanwhile, in the background, the senior champagne host Michael Donahue is hearing this entire conversation through a hidden camera he placed when the club was closed. He had seen the reservation earlier in the day for John Marino's party and brought in close friend and Silver Lights business contact, Eddie Maggio of New York City Confidential Security to help install hidden cameras in two areas, the VIP area near the stage, and the Howard Stern champagne room.

The hidden camera devices are small and barely noticeable to a human eye. He had Eddie Maggio connect the hidden camera app to his phone so Michael would be able to catch the high powered scandals going on, and use to his advantage.

Would Michael keep the hard evidence of this conversation sealed and let Sapphire Investments know his price to keep quiet about this , or would he go immediately to his long-time ally and close friend Brooks Kennedy and make a lucrative deal. The question that Michael Donahue faced was which deal would be the most lucrative and sound to keep him out jail.

In many ways, Michael's former white-collar crimes background made his role at Silver Lights lucrative because heavy hitters like Brooks Kennedy and John Marino would pay any price for hard evidence that could make or break the status of their firm.

PHILIP: I promise you it will be straightened out by next week.

JOHN: Another thing you may want to take in to consideration is to act overly nice to your wife. Shower her with affection, and it may have a better outcome. Try giving Cassandra roses and jewelry with a nice card. Small gestures go a long way, and she may confess to you before you end up spending a fortune with this firm.

The two settle up with the waitress, and Craig comes back with the girls. All the girls are making small talk as they head towards the dressing room and the gentlemen leave the club around 1:00 AM.

FADE OUT

ACT VI, SCENE 3
EVERYONE DANCES

INT: DRESSING ROOM

FADE IN

House Mom Shay is singing in the background to her Latin pop music and adhering to the nightly checkout procedures for the early girls who arrived before 6:00 PM for the first round of night cuts. She notices all three girls giggling and having fun.

SHAY: It looks like someone had a good night.

LOLA: It hasn't been a bad night, but money has been slow.

SHAY: How so?

LOLA: It was a bit empty tonight with the debates in the city and the basketball games.

SHAY: Makes sense.

LOLA: Tomorrow should be poppin' because we are getting two big customers, Steven Banks, and Brooks Kennedy. Both pay top money, but Steven is definitely easier to please. (*Giggles.*)

BRIANA: Brooks Kennedy can be a royal pain in the ass!

A voice from the other side of the dressing room, from someone who appears to look like Anastasia, says "Brooks is my customer." She comes towards the girls and Skylar is in disbelief that it is, in fact, Anastasia. She tries to play it cool.

SKYLAR: Anastasia . . .

ANASTASIA: Skylar. I thought that was you, but I told myself I may have had too much to drink tonight and saw someone that resembled you. Call me Elizabeth here.

SKYLAR: My name is Soleil here.

ANASTASIA: What in the world are you—

SKYLAR: Doing here? Some financial problems called the Big Apple Diet. And you?

ANASTASIA: I don't want to say much.

LOLA: You guys know each other?

SKYLAR: Yes, we work together in real estate.

BRIANNA: Small world. I'm assuming you guys are friends. It just reaffirms my theory that most people have double lives, and most dancers are normal girls that have jobs, go to school, or own a business.

Anastasia shifts her personality to a colder demeanor towards Skylar.

ANASTASIA: Yes, dancing is more common today with one job often times not being enough to meet one's basic finances, especially in such an expensive city.

BRIANNA: You still haven't answered my question, are you guys good friends?

ANASTASIA: I have seen her around in the office. Just casual acquaintances.

Skylar couldn't believe her ears. Was this the same woman who wanted updates on her listings, and her latest beaus, and diet tips? Anastasia would barge in every morning before she even had her coffee, asking her about leads and then being a pest about what she exactly ate to stay thin. It makes sense now why Anastasia had to worry about her waistline because she was dancing half-naked every night. It had nothing to do with her somewhat nerdy tech boyfriend Trey because he worshipped her. And the lies about looking good for an upcoming reunion were just a cover up for her role as an exotic dancer.

Skylar just decided to go along with the dialogue that they didn't know each other. There was obviously a reason Anastasia didn't want Lola and Brianna to know about their friendship, and the fact that Anastasia had said "Brooks is my customer" after hearing he was coming to the club tomorrow made Skylar think there was some type of rivalry between the two dancers?

So many thoughts were starting to run through Skylar's head.

Do dancers really have exclusivity on certain guys that walk through the doors? She thought the whole strip club idea was a way for men to escape the pressures of a girlfriend or wife and concentrate on enjoying themselves freely with whomever they desire. Just as Skylar was getting used to being Soleil, confusion started to enter her dialogue. She really did feel confident about her new role after nailing her performance on center stage and performing her first lap dance with Lola and John, but all of sudden she was lost for words.

LOLA: Soleil, are you ok? You look out of it.

SKYLAR: I'm fine. It's just been a long night, and I'm feeling a bit run down.

SHAY: Soleil, since it's your first night and you have been through a lot of firsts here, you can leave. Remember, your first week here, there will be no house fees and tip-outs unless you sell your first champagne room.

LOLA: She will be tipping out tomorrow, as she is my new protégé and will be in the champagne rooms with the foot monster, Steve Banks. Redmond paired her up with me this whole week.

Anastasia looks at Skylar with jealousy and a sense of betrayal. How was Skylar supposed to know that there was a rivalry between the girls? And what exactly was the rivalry about? Was it because Lola was the premiere seller and dancer at Silver Lights, or was there something more to the story?

SHAY: Soleil, you are honestly paired with one of the best dancers and sellers to ever walk through Silver Lights.

ANASTASIA: I have to get back to a customer. I will see you tomorrow. Have a good night.

BRIANNA: Girl, Brooks Kennedy is not her customer. He did one room with her a week ago for the first time in two years since I have been here, and she thinks it's her customer. I don't know what went down in the room, but he does rooms all the time with different girls.

SKYLAR: What makes a guy someone's customer? I thought the whole point of the establishment was for a guy to not feel like they are exclusive to one girl.

LOLA: Exactly, but if someone comes back to repeatedly see you or a specific dancer, and they spend a lot of time with you in the champagne rooms, then a dancer will often refer to them as their customer.

SKYLAR: Ok, that makes sense.

LOLA: So you're not close with Elizabeth, right?

SKYLAR: No, I am not. Why are you asking?

LOLA: She is not a team player in any situation. Don't trust her—she's a snitch. Just ask about every dancer here, she is seriously out for herself.

SKYLAR: Really? Well, I'm not that close with her. I just see her pass by in the office, that's all.

LOLA: She may look and act like Elle Woods from *Legally Blonde*, but she is the opposite. Everything that that comes out of her mouth ruins that "sweet as cherry pie" image.

SKYLAR: I can't believe what I'm hearing. I don't really know her well, but she appears fine at the office.

LOLA: Soleil, we are all here for one reason: to excel in our dreams. That can only happen if the fantasy runs somewhat smooth for the customer the moment they walk into Silver Lights until the time they leave. I'm warning you now, and don't tell me you didn't hear it. Stay clear of Elizabeth because the fantasy for both you and the customer will end up crashing. And when I say crashing, it has to do with not just your income, but your reputation. Do you get my drift?

SKYLAR: Yes, I hear you. I'm not going to be part of anything that ruins my income or jeopardizes my reputation at Silver Lights.

Skylar was speechless and she couldn't believe how deep the rivalry and drama went between these girls. On top of that, as if there weren't enough drama for one night, there were a few other dancers who felt the same way towards her friend from the office.

SHAY: Enough gossip, ladies! I need you girls, Bri and Lola, to finish up on the floor because Michael needs you. Skylar, I need to talk to you before you check out, and what to expect tomorrow with the porn star feature, Amber.

The two girls head out, and House Mom Shay's makeup looks radiant in the iridescent light, almost angelic.

SHAY: Skylar, sorry I didn't get your fingerprint earlier but I got tied up with some management issues. I need to get your fingerprint now and your picture for the system. Every time you come in to work, you're going to clock in and out with your fingerprint. You will have paid all your fees, redeemed your club dollars from any champagne bottles sold, and paid tip-outs to managers before clocking out. Let's do the fingerprint first.

Skylar gives House Mom Shay her right index finger, and she touches it to the keypad three times before it takes. Right before the picture, Skylar checks herself out as she appears a bit tired, but the red lipstick is still on.

SHAY: Smile, beautiful lady. (*Takes the picture.*) Great, that looks awesome. If you have a moment before you go, I just wanted to give you some advice.

SKYLAR: I'm all ears.

SHAY: Don't get caught up in the drama brewing within the club, especially the one that is starting to spotlight around your dancers about sex, drugs, and rock n' roll. There are always two sides to a story, so don't be biased towards one dancer over another. Just let the drama unfold, rather than be part of it.

SKYLAR: You mean the warning from Lola.

HOUSE MOM: I'm just saying don't get caught up in the drama of the club. I'm here to guide you, not to tell you what to do, and to remind you that when you walked through Silver Lights, You left a life of ordinary slippers in exchange for an exciting pair of sparkling *Silver Heels* that will keep you shining towards your dream.

THE GRAND FINALE

Those magnetic words, "Silver Heels that will keep you shining towards your dream," took hold of Skylar Lynn's entire mind, body, and spirit. You can see her aura became lighter as the cast of dark shadows began to fade away into her closing act. She began to inhale those powerful visions from her Playground of Dreams. For the second time in her life, as she began to meditate, by connecting her inhales and exhales to her mind, body, and spirit, she began to experience the same joy she had as a young kid with dreams that continued to flow in the direction of her Hollywood Dream. From the side mirror of the dressing room, a strobe of white light sparkled silver, radiating in both directions. The experience she felt again from The Silver Lights and with her meditation was so powerful that, for just a few seconds, she felt again the paranormal, out-of-body experience. The Light of Silver had touched Skylar Lynn's soul in such a moving way that giving birth to a new dialogue and dream was awaiting her with a set of swanky new Silver Heels in her second feature screenplay, Hollywood Dreams.

FADE OUT

SILVER HEELS:
THE SEQUEL TO SILVER LIGHTS.

Seven weeks have passed and Skylar Lynn's life of plain slippers and hot latte runs have been traded up for a life of sparkling Silver Heels and cool energy drinks. Since departing her first feature, *The City of Dreams*, she has danced her way into her second feature, *Hollywood Dreams* where the storylines are hotter, the dialogue is scandalous, and the characters are unpredictable. In her second screenplay, *Hollywood Dreams*, she portrays a sultry dancer that conflicts with her role as "Skylar." In her most foreign role yet, the question becomes will Skylar be able to push through her first two acts in her debut screenplay, *Hollywood Dreams* with ease and conviction as "Soleil", the Exotic Dancer or will she go back to a life of slippers and lattes?.

Both the new age drama of *Silver Heels* and the screenplay *Hollywood Dreams* will take you into the darkest scenes of organized crime, the dialogue of Wall Street scandals and a forbidden love affair, as aspiring Hollywood star, Skylar Lynn, continues to capture her authentic voice, never losing sight of her dreams that one day she will shine at the Golden Globes, as she gives you her most riveting drama yet in her second screenplay, *Hollywood Dreams*.

ABOUT THE AUTHOR

Michelle Lynn is an author, actress, painter, and health founder of The Zen Food Diet. When she is not working on writing, painting, or film projects with The Michelle Lynn Brand, or cooking up her signature health recipes, you can find her traveling to tropical destinations, practicing yoga, dancing, writing, attending health events, and taking long runs along the beach.

She resides in both Austin, Texas and South Florida, and travels regularly to New York City and Los Angeles for on-camera work, acting, writing, fitness modeling, blogging projects, and creative development. She has already published two books in lifestyle and cooking, as *The Food Orgy Book Series™. A Tropical Fantasy, A Sensual Guide to Healthy Living and The Chocolate Orgy, A Dating Guide To Cooking up Bittersweet Endings* are both are available on Amazon.com

Made in the USA
Coppell, TX
19 March 2020

17204960R00095